TORNADO WARNING

The Damaged Climate Series Book 1

J.R. TATE

RustyBucket Publishing

This book is a work of fiction and is for your personal enjoyment only. Any similarities to names, places, or events are coincidental. This book may not be resold or given away to another person. It may not be transmitted in any way without written permission from the author.

Copyright © 2016 by Rusty Bucket Publishing

Cover art by J.R. Tate

Books available in The Damaged Climate Series:

Tornado Warning (Book One)

Drought Warning (Book Two)

Blizzard Warning (Book Three)

❦ Created with Vellum

ALSO BY J.R. TATE

Respect the Wind Series

Fury - Book One

Rage - Book 2

The Defiants Series

Inception - Book One

Captive - Book Two

Desist - Book Three

The Firefighter Heroes Series

Through Smoke - Book One

Backfire - Book Two

Fire Escape - Book Three

The Gifted Curse Series

Beckoning Souls - Book One

Wayward Souls - Book Two

ALSO BY J.R. TATE (CONTINUED)

Stand-Alone Novels

Fade to Gray

Reformed

Keep the Wolves Away

Dangerous Betrayal

Murphy's War

CHAPTER ONE

Looking back now, they should have seen it coming. With advanced technology and accurate forecasting, it should have never played out the way it had. As the old cliché went – hindsight is twenty-twenty, and what Ryan Gibson would have done to go back and change everything. The difference of a few seconds would've altered the outcome of everything that had happened.

"I REALLY WISH you didn't have to work today, Ry." Cecilia Gibson flipped the pancake on the griddle and tightened her bathrobe around her midsection. Arching her eyebrow, she poured herself a cup of coffee and smirked. "It's already bad enough that we don't see you when you get called in. I know volunteering at the fire department is something you've always wanted to do. It just pulls you away at the worst times."

"It's not like we get tons of calls, hon. And this is one Saturday out of the month that I have to go into the shop. It's my turn. You know, my actual real job as a mechanic that pays the bills. Next week it'll be Danny's and his wife will be the one complaining." Winking, he ruffled his hand through his son's hair. "How's the pancakes, Ty?"

The child shook his head and gave a thumbs up, his mouth full of food, and a small drop of syrup fell to his chin.

"You got a five-year-old's stamp of approval, hon." Ryan wrapped his arm around Cecilia's waist, pulling her in for a hug, her back pressed into him. "I'll be home early. There wasn't much on the list when I left yesterday. Sometimes Saturdays are busy with walk-ins, so we'll see. I'll let you know."

"The National Weather Service is anticipating that a tornado watch will be issued later this afternoon for several counties in the area. A weather system is brewing over the mountains and will impact us tonight. Keep it tuned here for updates."

Ryan and Cecilia turned to the television, and she patted his arm. "Busy this morning at the shop. Busy tonight with the fire department. No, you don't get a ton of fires, but they always want the volunteers to go out and watch the weather. And according to the meteorologist on channel five, it's going to be a hell of a storm season. Ty and I may never see you."

Ryan leaned in and kissed her on the lips. "You know the nickname of the meteorologist on channel five, don't you?"

"No. Do I wanna know?"

"Doomsday Donald. You know how the man makes things worse than they are. About the only damn thing he gets right is the wind. Don't worry! We'll grill those steaks when I get home tonight. You know what'd be really nice?" His eyes widened and he didn't give her a chance to answer. "It'd be awesome if you'd do those bacon-wrapped cheese stuffed peppers to go with it. What do you say?"

"Get to work!" She pecked him on the lips again, walking with him to the door. "Love you, babe."

"Love you."

Ryan climbed into his pickup and merged onto the highway. There was definitely a change in the air, and he parked the truck on the side of the road, watching the clouds coming over the top of the distant mountains on the horizon. As a volunteer firefighter, he was required to take storm spotting classes, and he had just taken a refresher course a few months ago. A tornado watch was possible, but it was nothing out of the ordinary. It was a little early, with storm season not usually starting for a while, but it was Texas – the weather was always unpredictable.

Drumming his thumb on the steering wheel, he took in the spectacular view. The sky was purple and orange against the sunrise, and the humidity was thick. The atmosphere was favorable for some storms and Ryan couldn't wait – there was nothing like a large system coming through, with lightning flashing, and thunder roaring, as long as the severe stuff stayed away from the populated areas.

Watching for a few more minutes, he headed into town. It was a ten-mile drive from his place out in the county, and it gave him time to wake up on the way in, and wind down on the way home.

The population sign on the edge of Harper Springs read a little over a thousand people. The rural county was home to mostly farming families, and though sometimes the monotony was unbearable, Ryan couldn't think of anywhere else he'd want to live. Everyone knew him and it was comforting to think about the tight-knit community where he had grown up.

Waving toward Mrs. McElroy, he could smell the fresh donuts in her bakery located right next door to the mechanic shop. She left the door wide open on purpose as a marketing ploy to pull in customers. She had the best coffee and baked goods in town.

Parking his truck, Ryan slid out and tipped the brim of his baseball cap. "Good morning, Mrs. McElroy. Sure smells delicious in there."

"Just made some fresh cinnamon rolls. I even iced some in chocolate. You ought to come grab a couple. Aren't those your favorite?"

Ryan patted his stomach and smiled. "Cecilia made pancakes.

Had I known you were gonna ice the cinnamon rolls in chocolate, I would've saved some room."

Mrs. McElroy wagged her finger at him. "You know good and well that I do it every Saturday. I've been doing it since you were about this tall." She motioned her hand close to the ground and laughed. "So, it's your Saturday to work, huh? Got a lot going on?"

"A few oil changes and flats, but nothing too horrible."

"Good. You don't need to be in town late anyway. Supposed to be storms tonight."

"You've been watching Doomsday Donald too, huh?"

Mrs. McElroy folded her arms over her chest. "I'm sixty-three years old, Ryan Gibson. Lived in Harper Springs every one of them. I can feel it in the air. We've had some big ones come through and we're overdue for another."

"You think so?" Ryan cocked his head to the side and adjusted his baseball cap. The temperature was starting to heat up and he wiped some sweat from his brow.

"How old are you, Ryan?"

"I'll be thirty-seven in April."

"And you've lived all thirty-seven here too, right?"

He scoffed and edged toward his shop. If he wanted to get home at a decent time, he'd need to get to work. "I see where you're going with this, Mrs. McElroy. I know how the weather is, Ma'am. I'm not saying we'll never get another big one, but I don't think it's gonna be tonight."

"Maybe not tonight, but soon. You tell your daddy hello for me, okay?"

"Yes Ma'am, I'll do that. I might hop over later for some coffee and one of those cinnamon rolls."

Unlocking the garage, he skimmed his finger down the work order log. Just as he anticipated – three oil changes, a tire change, and one brake replacement. Depending on if anyone walked in, he would be done in a few hours. Starting on the first car, he went to work, halfway listening to the radio as he focused on the first car. His mind was on Mrs. McElroy's prediction. Hopefully, it would be an active season. The last few had been a bust, and he was ready to see some good weather come through.

"The steaks were fantastic, hon." Ryan sat beside Cecilia on the couch. The TV was on, but he wasn't paying attention to it. Clasping his fingers in hers, he closed his eyes, relaxing into the cushions as he drifted off. She tightened her grip on him and leaned in, kissing him.

"You cooked them. I can't take all of your glory."

Opening one of his eyes, he glanced at her. "You didn't have to make the peppers. I know they're a pain in the ass."

"I've had to make them so much, it's no problem. Besides, now you owe me."

Sitting up, Ryan nudged her. "Yeah? What do you have in mind?"

"I'm not sure. I'll have to think about it, and I won't forget, so don't count on that."

"Oh, I know you won't forget. You're still ruminating on crap that happened when we first got married. If there's one thing I've learned about you, it's that you've got a hell of a memory."

"We are interrupting the scheduled broadcast for a severe weather report. The National Weather Service has issued a tornado warning for Grant County, including the city of Fox Lake. Residents are urged to take cover immediately, as our storm chaser has spotted a tornado on the ground about ten miles southwest of the city, moving northeast."

"Fox Lake?" Cecilia grabbed her phone, her eyes wide. "You think my parents are seeing this?"

"Call them, but make it quick. Probably shouldn't be on the phone for very long."

Ryan sat up and looked out the front living room window. Fox Lake was about sixty miles away and to the north, so they were out of harm's way, but Cecilia's parents and some of her family lived there. Stepping out onto the porch, he watched the twisting and churning of clouds. There was a drastic temperature change from the mid-eighties to the sixties, dipping twenty degrees in a matter of a few minutes.

Looking to the north, the tail end of the storm impacting Grant County lit up as lightning flashed from cloud to cloud, the thunderhead so massive that it looked like an atomic bomb had been dropped.

"They said they were in their cellar. Did they even issue a tornado watch?" Cecilia joined him on the porch, still clutching her cell phone.

"I didn't even pay attention. Maybe it'll miss them." He pointed toward the top of the thunderhead. "See what looks like an anvil at the top?"

Cecilia nodded. Her brow creased with worry as she looked where he was pointing.

"If you watch that, it'll tell you which way the storm is going. Right now, it's going northeast, but by the angle, it looks like it may make a more eastern track, and if that's the case, your parents should be okay. There's nothing south of Fox Lake, so if it goes that way, it'll just hit some open farmland."

"I hope you're right, Ry."

A flash of lightning and an instant clap of thunder rumbled nearby, and they went back inside, slamming the door. "Holy shit, that came out of nowhere." Grabbing his scanner, he turned it on. No one had paged him to get out and storm spot, but maybe someone in Grant County was out and reporting the situation. There was nothing but dead air and Ryan focused back on the TV.

"We are hearing reports that Fox Lake and Grant County are without power. We are unable to make contact with our storm chaser, but we are tracking the supercell on the Doppler, and it looks to miss Fox Lake to the south."

Cecilia relaxed some, but she didn't move from the front of the television. Ryan scanned the frequencies on the scanner, only able to pick up bits and pieces of conversations, most from departments not related to Grant County and Fox Lake. Their electricity flickered but stayed on, and Ty stood at the foot of the stairs, clutching a stuffed teddy bear, rubbing his eyes.

"Daddy, I'm scared." He was still half asleep, but another flash of lightning and rumble of thunder shook the whole house, making him jump into Ryan's arms.

"It's just a storm, Ty. Everything will be okay."

"It's loud. How come it's not raining?"

Ryan didn't answer his son. He continued to try and find a weather report but was unsuccessful. It was a typical storm for the area, mainly electrical with high winds and a small sprinkling of rain, but with Cecilia's family possibly in the path, there was a sense of urgency to find out more.

"The National Weather Service has now downgraded the storm in Grant County to a thunderstorm warning. It is still very dangerous, but we are happy to report that it missed Fox Lake and is now dissipating."

"Oh, thank God!" Cecilia laughed and took Ty from Ryan. "I'll give it a few more minutes and try to call them to make sure. You were right, Ryan. I guess those storm spotting classes are paying off."

Ryan went back on the porch. The dark clouds were fading, and he could see a few stars showing through the haze. Doomsday Donald had been right – was this a small preview of what was to come? At least everyone had dodged a bullet. The smell of rain was refreshing, and it began to pour, splattering the wood at his feet. Rolling thunder and distant lightning accompanied the rainfall, downgrading the severity to just a typical springtime weather pattern.

"Okay. Good. I'm glad y'all were able to get down into the cellar. I'm sure there will be plenty of insurance agents in the area." Cecilia nodded to Ryan, holding Ty in one arm as she cradled her phone against her ear. All the tension on her face was gone. "Okay, Mom. Love you too. We'll come by tomorrow." She ended the call and slid the phone into her pocket.

"Well?" Ryan stepped forward, offering to take Ty, but the child had his face buried in Cecilia's neck, unwilling to move.

"They got some hail and a little damage, but the house is fine. Can't say the same about Dad's truck."

"That's good. That was a nasty storm. They were lucky."

"I told them we'd come over tomorrow. Things might look different when the sun comes up."

Ryan nodded. "Sure. Anything we can do to help." Turning his attention back out into the yard, he took in the fresh rain scent and humidity on his skin. "Sure is beautiful, isn't it?" Glancing over his shoulder, he noticed he was alone. Cecilia had taken Ty back inside. Leaning on the porch railing, he skimmed his hand through some rain that had pooled on the wood. Mrs. McElroy's words echoed in his head – they were overdue for another big one. Tonight wasn't the night. Maybe this year wouldn't be the year.

CHAPTER TWO

"It got my truck and I'm pretty sure we'll need to call a roofer. Past that, we haven't been outside to look at the rest of the damage." Charlie Johnson sat at the kitchen table, inviting Ryan, Cecilia, and Ty to have breakfast with them. "How'd it look driving from Harper Springs?" Ryan was thankful he got along with his in-laws and Ty adored his grandparents. It was always nice to see them, even if it was for unfortunate circumstances.

"It looks like you might've lost a few windows on the south side, but it was hard to tell. There were some trees down as we got closer to Fox Lake, but not near what I expected. I'm sure it was worse in the southern part of the county," Ryan replied as he helped Cecilia's mother serve a plate for Ty.

"Have they said how big it was?" Margaret Johnson finished breakfast and joined them at the table.

"No ma'am. I haven't heard anything. Probably will be a few days. They have to look at the damage and things." Ryan dipped a strip of bacon in his egg yolk. "I'm sure they're going to need our department to go help if anyone got hurt. There aren't too many towns between here and there, so maybe everyone was safe."

"Well, Ryan, how about we go outside and see what we can fix? They're forecasting another system like last night that could come through again. We at least need to get the broken windows boarded up until we can get them replaced."

Ty joined them and was happy to be given a rubber mallet to keep him occupied as Ryan and Charlie analyzed the damage. Every window on the south side was broken or cracked, and some of the siding had been beaten off from hail. Ryan had brought some plywood from his place, but it wasn't enough to fix each window. He counted six total, thankful that it had just impacted the south side of the house.

Measuring the size of the windows, each one was about the same, and he placed some wood on two sawhorses. It was a little after eight AM and the heat had climbed into the nineties. The humidity was thick enough to cut through, and he brushed his forearm over his face to keep the sweat from dripping into his eyes. Charlie steadied the wood as Ryan powered up the saw, slicing the plywood where he had measured.

He took a short break and drank two glasses of iced tea and went back to work. He never panicked about the weather. It was pointless to fret over something they had no control over, and more times than not, the forecast was a bust. But Charlie Johnson was an old timer and another person who had lived in the area a long time. His concern was valid, and Ryan wasn't going to argue with getting the needed repairs done in case they had a repeat and weren't so lucky the next time.

"I've got some more plywood out in the barn. It should be enough to finish up the last two windows." Charlie's eyes looked past Ryan toward the mountain range. "Same clouds as yesterday. I must've sat out here for an hour watching it. Yesterday it was beautiful. Today, I'm not as happy to see it."

Ryan followed his gaze. It was the same thing he had watched on the side of the highway when driving to work. It was the dry line, already setting up to the west. If it became active and retreated, the storms would fire up in no time. Maybe calling the local meteorologist Doomsday Donald was a bit premature, but he shook it off. He'd seen the dry line set up like that many times, bringing beneficial rainfall to the area. He wasn't going to let himself get lost in the hype of another potentially severe night. He was going to prepare and be ready.

Cecilia stepped out onto the back porch, tossing them both a bottle of water. "Your favorite meteorologist just said that we're in for it again."

Ryan nailed up the last piece of plywood and hopped down from the ladder. "How's the barns look?" He glanced up at Cecilia, and though he wasn't ignoring her, he didn't have much to say. All the talk about the weather was going to freak Ty out, and thankfully he was busy playing, his attention on something else.

"Not bad. They've got some damage, but nothing we need to worry about right now." Charlie patted him on the shoulder. "Thanks for the help. I would've never gotten that done by myself."

"No problem. Makes me wonder if I need to go ahead and board up my windows just in case. Like those folks in Florida and on the coast have to do with hurricane warnings. I'll go home and do it and not a damn thing will happen."

Charlie laughed and shook his head. "I don't know, Ryan. I've seen my fair share of this stuff, but something in the air feels different. We're not even out of February yet and we're setting records for highs. With daytime heating, all the atmosphere has to do is organize and ramp up."

"Don't tell me you're one of those global warming fanatics, Charlie. I thought you were as conservative as they come." Ryan laughed and sipped on his water.

"I don't think the climate is changing. I just think we're cycling, and right now, we're in a pretty bad one. And it's time. The past few years have been calm storm seasons. Last night I swear we had softball-sized hail. I couldn't get too close to the window, but just look at my truck."

The windows were shattered, and the roof was completely smashed. "And that's from the main part of the storm missing you. Makes you wonder how big the hail was in the main core." Ryan walked to the end of the truck bed and whistled. "Definitely softball-sized, at least."

"Call me crazy, Ryan, but you don't seem too concerned."

"It's not that. I just don't like the media hype. That meteorologist, Donald whatever his name is, is known for going with the weather models that are on the highest end of extreme. It's concerning that today is starting as a carbon copy of yesterday, but I can't worry about it. What are we gonna do about it? Put giant walls up to keep the twisters out?"

Charlie tried to pull the tailgate down, but the damage hindered it from moving. "You got your cellar stocked up?"

"Not how we should, no. I guess it's ready to go if you like wine."

Charlie didn't find it amusing, and his brow furrowed. "When you leave here today, go buy some canned goods and nonperishable items. Being prepared doesn't mean you're giving in to the hype. It means you've got my daughter and my grandson on your mind, and I know damn well they are the world to you. You'll do everything you can to protect them. And hey, if it's a bust, that's why you get the foods that don't go bad really fast."

Ryan nodded. "Yes sir, you're right." Deep down, he knew it was something to take seriously. His instincts were screaming at him, telling him that it would get worse, and though he was denying it, keeping it buried would never stop the potential freight train that could soon be barreling toward them.

Charlie was right about several things – Cecilia and Ty were Ryan's main priorities, and stocking up the cellar would be the first line of defense in keeping them safe.

CHAPTER TWO

"I thought you weren't getting into the weather hype!" Cecilia nudged Ryan as he pulled into the parking lot of the grocery store. "What exactly did you boys talk about when you were patching up the windows?"

Ryan put the truck in gear and glanced over his shoulder at Ty. He had fallen asleep in an awkward position, his mouth wide open and a faint snore escaping his nose. Good thing he was asleep – Ryan didn't want to talk about it in front of him.

"He suggested getting some food for the cellar. It's not a bad idea. I always planned to do it, but just like with everything else, I never got around to it."

"He thinks we're in for some big stuff, doesn't he?" Cecilia cocked her eyebrow and looked at Ty.

"Just like all the old timers around here, saying we're overdue for another big one. I'm no meteorologist, so I can't say they're wrong. And like your dad said, get food that doesn't go bad fast. No harm in being prepared."

Cecilia unbuckled her seatbelt and opened the truck door. "This, coming from a guy who was making fun of the man on channel five."

Ryan ignored her comment and picked Ty up, allowing him to sleep on his shoulder. The boy stirred for a moment, mumbling something, his body like dead weight as he drifted back to sleep. Setting him in the basket, Ryan wondered how many people in the store were doing the same thing they were. Were they keeping an eye on the weather, or were they completely unaware of the possibility of an outbreak of storms? The chances of anything detrimental happening were slim, and though Ryan hated cliches, it was better safe than sorry.

"So, what do you wanna stock up on?" Ryan avoided the produce and meat section. "Canned ravioli and spaghettios for our youngster." He held up the cans and placed them in the basket. "Ever try canned tamales?"

Cecilia wrinkled her nose. "I guess if I'm hungry enough, I'll eat them."

Ryan grabbed a couple of bags of flour, some sugar, and some bottled water. He also got some fire logs – they'd be handy in case they lost power. He had plenty of firewood from the past winter that they didn't use, and the fire logs would help get a good burn going. He was certain he was missing something. What else would be useful?

Batteries and a couple of extra flashlights would be nice to have to accompany the propane lanterns he had in the garage. Extra bottles of propane would be good since the camping stove was also powered by it. He made a mental note to make sure to move all the camping gear to the cellar.

Reaching for a cheap bag of coffee, Cecilia laughed and pointed. "Somehow I knew you couldn't pass up on that."

"We've got a campfire percolator. Might as well buy the cheap stuff that a spoon will stand up in for the real effect."

Ty began to wake up, his eyes widening when he saw they were in the store. "I want some candy. Mommy, can I have some candy?"

"We're not here for our usual groceries, hon. But look, we got the ravioli you like so much."

Ty's smile beamed and he lifted a couple of the cans to look at them. "I want gummy bears. Can I have some gummy bears?"

Ryan tossed an assortment bag full of candy bars into the basket, avoiding Cecilia's glare. What was the point if they couldn't enjoy a delicious snack amid all of the canned, processed food that in no way seemed appetizing? For safe measure, he handed Ty a bag of gummy bears, winking at his son.

"Think we about covered everything?" Ryan asked as they went to the checkout lines.

Cecilia looked over the items. "I guess so. I've never had to do this kind of shopping, but it should hold us over if we..." she stopped herself, smiling at Ty. "Yeah. It's good. If we think of anything else, we can come back."

The cashier rang them up and snapped his gum between his

teeth. A smirk pursed his lips, and he looked up at Ryan. "There a zombie apocalypse coming that I don't know about?"

Ryan's face heated up. "What?"

"Nothing. No one likes this." He held up the can of tamales and winced. "Don't worry. I'm a certified zombie killer. I got the bumper sticker on my car to prove it." The teenager laughed and continued to ring up the groceries.

Ryan wasn't amused. He felt like a jackass, but when they walked out to the truck, the thick air made his decision to stock up on nonperishables feel justified. The mountain range to the west was serving as a perfect vantage point to watch the instability in the atmosphere form, and towers were already starting to pop up. Soon, the small cloud formation would erupt into large thunderheads much like the atomic-like clouds he watched the night before.

Cecilia was quiet on the drive home, and Ty was busy playing with a toy in the backseat, in his own little world where Ryan hoped he'd stay. The kid got scared any time a storm came through. How would he handle a tornado?

"I'll get all of this down in the cellar. I wanna pull the camping stuff out and see what we have."

"Go inside and wash your hands, Ty. I'll make you a snack." Turning back to Ryan, she grabbed his hand and squeezed. "Everything will be fine."

"I know. Your dad just got me thinking."

"He tends to do that. I'm gonna go inside and help Ty. Let me know if you need anything." She leaned in and pecked him on the cheek, her smile calming Ryan's nerves.

Ryan carried the bags of groceries down into the cellar, the musty scent nauseating. Pulling the light on, he skimmed his fingers through the dust that had collected on the shelves. He had eight bottles of different types of wine on a shelf – some of them representing special occasions. Lifting a bottle of Moscato, he reminisced about his and Cecilia's wedding day. He had to hide the bottle from everyone at the reception, and fifteen years later, he still had it, just waiting for the perfect moment to open it.

Sliding it back on the shelf, he put the bags of groceries nearby, not even bothering to organize them. The cellar wasn't the cleanest place, and he wanted to make sure all his camping gear was in working order.

Getting back to ground level, the sudden change in barometric pressure took his breath away, and his head felt like it was going to explode. Looking toward the mountains, the towers he had just watched were huge, darkening the sky like it was nighttime. Trees swayed in the wind, and the temperature must have dropped about fifteen degrees within minutes. The sky held a green hue, which meant hail was on the way.

Hurrying inside, he flipped it to a local TV station.

"A tornado watch has been issued for all the viewing area. A fast-developing squall line will be moving across the area as an outflow will force the dry line to retreat. We are dealing with a very unstable atmosphere, so please keep it here, and we'll let you know of any warnings or danger that may arise from this ominous storm system."

Ryan couldn't take his eyes off the screen as he watched the Doppler change each time it swept over the storms.

"Ryan, you gonna answer that?" Cecilia pointed at his cell phone on the table. He didn't realize it had been ringing until she broke his concentration.

"This is Gibson."

"Gibson, it's Lieu."

"Hey, Lieutenant Cannady."

"Are you able to go out and spot? I'm trying to get all the guys out there. It's looking pretty rough, and we need as many eyes on the storm as possible to relay back to town."

Ryan didn't answer at first. His attention was on Cecilia and Ty. He debated on leaving them, but he also had a duty with the fire department. He could storm spot until the severe stuff got close to home, then come back and make sure they were safe.

"Yeah, Lieu. Let me get with Cecilia and I'll call you back." He hung up the phone and slipped it in his pocket.

Cecilia folded her arms over her chest and bit her bottom lip. She knew exactly what that phone call was about. "They want you to go chase, don't they?"

CHAPTER THREE

Ryan thought long and hard before deciding to go chase. He had a responsibility to his family and one to the fire department, and since the storm looked to be tracking west of their area, he decided to go chase for a while. He'd keep Cecilia informed and told her to keep the scanner on. Any word of it getting remotely close and she was to take Ty down into the cellar and not come out until things cleared up.

Taking the highway south, his best bet was to come in behind the storm. That was where the strongest part would be, and he wouldn't get stuck in a hail shaft or a rain-wrapped tornado if he stayed back. It was also the best way he had learned to find out which way it was moving.

Rain had already come through and the roadway was wet. Slowing his speed, he made sure not to hydroplane. He spotted the hail shaft immediately. It didn't appear to be over a populated area, but he radioed in what he was seeing.

"There is a hail shaft on the south side of the storm. Looks to still be moving more northward, and right now it is over some farmland."

"10-4, Gibson. What is your position?" Lieutenant Cannady's voice shook.

CHAPTER THREE

"I'm on Highway Five to the south, coming up right behind it."

"What's the damage look like?"

"There are some tree limbs down and the hail on the side of the road looks like it snowed out here. We've got some farmers who will probably need to get out here and count their cattle. Storm looks to be strengthening as it moves north. No towns in its path, but if it holds together, Roger's Pass will be under the gun."

"Copy, Gibson. Thanks."

Ryan put the radio in the passenger seat and watched the sky. There wasn't much traffic out, but the vehicles that were passing him flashed their lights and honked, probably thinking he was a moron for driving toward the natural disaster.

Pulling his phone out, he snapped a couple of pictures. He had seen some massive storms, but this one was a beauty, as long as it stayed away from towns. Slowing his truck to almost a stop, he pulled to the side of the highway and rolled his window down. The air was cold, almost like winter, matching the hail caught in the grass, appearing as if it had snowed. It looked like softball sized had come through, and a nearby barn had been slammed – the metal siding had huge dents and the roof was caved in on the south side.

Gripping the steering wheel, Ryan second-guessed himself. He was a trained storm spotter but had never been through on a storm of that caliber. The air was damp, and a hint of spring blew in the wind. The sky was an ominous green mixed with gray, and the trees whipped around. Rain splattered his windshield, but it was quick, and it stopped just as fast as it had started.

An SUV came up behind him, traveling fast, but slowed as it approached him. There were two occupants inside, a male and a female, and the passenger side window rolled down as they pulled up next to Ryan's truck. The side of the car said something about The National Weather Service, and with the radio antenna and weather gadgets, it didn't take a genius to realize they were professional storm chasers.

"You need help, sir?" The man leaned over the console and yelled across.

"No. I'm with the local fire department. Out spotting for Harper Springs."

"Looks like it'll miss you. But I wouldn't sit here too long."

Ryan sat up in his seat. "Why's that? We're not safe behind it?"

"It looks like we've got a back-tracker. The anvil has shifted, and it's going to turn and come back southwest."

Ryan's heart skipped a beat, and he gripped the steering wheel. They were sitting right in its path, and as the storm chaser had predicted, the darkness was getting closer, coming right back down Highway Five.

He didn't have a chance to say anything to the chasers. Precipitation began to pick up, hindering his view out of the front window. In seconds, the hail shaft would be there, so he did a fast U-turn and slammed his foot on the accelerator, flooring the pickup. The engine revved and the RPMs shot to the max, his tires skidding in the water that pooled on the road. He saw the SUV in front of him, but the red taillights disappeared in the sheets of horizontal rain.

He was going almost 100 miles per hour, but it still wasn't fast enough to escape the storm that was right on his heels. It was so dark that if the storm was tornadic, there was no way for him to know. His radio crackled in the seat next to him, but he didn't have a chance to answer it. If he took one hand off the steering wheel, he'd lose control of his truck.

Hail came next, and it fell in shards. Unclassifiable sizes like broken glass, hammering his truck, damaging it like it was a crumpled can of soda. It was demolishing anything that was in its path.

Ryan looked to his left and saw the largest tornado he had ever seen. The only thing he could think to do was go the opposite direction again, and he turned down a farm-to-market road. It was the only chance he had to get away before the storm completely consumed him.

CECILIA MADE sure that Ty wasn't in the room. The scanner was going crazy with multiple spotters reporting what they were seeing, but where in the hell was Ryan? He had just spoken to Lieutenant Cannady and then he was gone. The guys had called him several times, but he didn't respond.

Keeping the volume on the TV low, she took a deep breath when the weatherman mentioned that the storm was backtracking. Didn't Ryan say he was south of it? Skimming her fingers through her hair, she sat on the edge of the coffee table and kept her eyes on the report.

"Gibson, come in!"

Dead air. Why wasn't he answering? Grabbing her phone, she dialed his number, but it went straight to voicemail. He was never one to be diligent about answering it, but his lack of response on the radio triggered her worry, and she took a deep breath to calm her racing heart. It was one thing to ignore a phone call, but he never ignored the fire department on the radio.

She paced down the hallway because it was the only thing she could think to do. She couldn't go out and look for him – there was no way in hell she'd take Ty out in it. She couldn't call Lieutenant Cannady or Chief Rayburn. They were far too busy making sure Harper Springs was safe.

"Mommy, what's wrong?" Ty stuck his head out of his room. At five years old, the boy was very observant.

"Nothing, baby. There's a big storm and I'm just watching it on TV." Cecilia pointed toward the television and forced a smile.

"Is daddy out there in it?"

She couldn't lie to him. "Yes. He's out there watching it, Ty."

She bit her bottom lip and felt the burn in her eyes. "Go back to your room and play. I'm about to make you a snack."

His eyebrows lifted and his eyes widened. Thank goodness it was easy to transition him to something else and get his mind off reality. But the boy was smart. He knew what was going on, even if he didn't ask any more questions.

She focused back on the weather report but couldn't hear what the meteorologist was saying over the radio traffic on the scanner. Every time someone relayed what they were seeing, she hoped it would be Ryan, but he still hadn't answered when they called for him. Pulling herself into the kitchen, she watched the sky from the window over the sink. It was dark and rotating, but moving away.

She grabbed her phone again and dialed her parents. As unpredictable as everything had been, she had no clue if Fox Lake was under the gun. Her father answered after the second ring, settling her nerves.

"Hey, Dad. Are y'all okay?"

"We're fine. I was about to call you. How's the weather there?"

Cecilia sat at the kitchen table and blinked back the warmth in the corner of her eyes. "Just rained a little here. Nothing else. Ryan had to go chase. His lieutenant called and needed some guys out there."

"Everything okay? You sound like you're on the verge of crying."

So much for hiding her emotions. "He's not answering anyone on the radio."

"Ryan isn't?"

"No, Dad. He was there, and then the storm shifted, and now he's not. I can't get him to answer his cell phone either. I'm worried. He was just south of it, and then it backtracked toward him."

There was a short pause, and the silence made the knot in

her stomach grow. "I'm sure he's fine. I heard that signal has been lost in those areas. Maybe his radio isn't working."

"I want to think that's what happened, but I just... I don't know."

She leaned back in her chair, and Ty joined her in the kitchen. Before he could say anything, she grabbed a cookie from the pantry and poured him a glass of milk, quickly appeasing him before he hammered her with more questions. Glancing out of the window again, she wished the storm would be completely gone, but the sky was still as dark as night.

"While I have you on the phone, I'll let you know that we did get the cellar stocked up."

"Good! I was worried that y'all weren't taking this seriously."

Cecilia forced a smile. "Lots of spam, beef jerky, canned fruit, and vegetables. I hope to God we'll never have to live off it. There's a reason I don't usually buy that crap. We're so used to the fresh stuff."

"I hope we won't have to either."

She opened her mouth to say something else, but the rumble of a truck interrupted her train of thought, and she ran to the living room, swinging the door open. Ryan's pickup was coming down the drive.

"Dad, I gotta go. Ryan made it home. I'll call you later to check in."

She ended the call and ran down the steps, meeting him in the driveway. The windshield was smashed and almost gone, and smoke billowed from under the hood. The dents in the vehicle were bigger than anything she had ever seen, like a giant had slammed his foot on top of it. But what caught her attention the most was the gaze on Ryan's face – unemotional and flat as he parked the truck.

"Ryan... are you okay?"

It took him a second to get out. Swinging the door open, the hinges squeaked. There was blood on his forehead from a gash right under his hairline.

"Ryan? What happened?"

He shook his head and looked up at the sky. "I'm not sure what the hell I just saw."

"What do you mean?" She ran her index finger near the wound. It looked like it might need stitches.

"I'm just glad it didn't hit us. That it didn't get near Harper Springs." He swiped his hand across his forehead, smearing the blood. "One second, I was behind it, safe, and then it's like it got slammed in reverse and came right at me. Like I was playing chicken with it or something."

"I'm glad you made it home."

"Barely. I've never seen anything like it. Pieces of hail as big as my head. It was like a war movie, and we were under attack. I saw some storm chasers right before the storm shifted. I never saw them after that. I don't know if they made it. And the truck..." He motioned toward it, ducking his head. "There's no way I'll be able to salvage it. I didn't think I'd get it back here."

"That's okay, Ryan. You're home and safe. Though I think you might need to have that looked at."

He touched his forehead again and wiped the blood on his pants. "Compliments of the windshield. I swear a hailstone the size of a cow came down and did that. But I'm fine. I'm sure the hospitals are packed with people who need help more than I do."

"At least let me clean it up and make sure there isn't any glass in it. If it is still bleeding in a little bit, we're going to the ER."

He followed her into the house, ducking past Ty's room before he saw his dad that way. Grabbing some hydrogen peroxide and some cotton balls, she motioned toward the edge of the bed. Surprisingly, Ryan wasn't putting up too much of a fight. Either he was too tired, or he knew they needed to take care of the injury.

Dabbing the cotton ball in the medicine, she gently ran it across the cut. Ryan cringed and closed his eyes, and the liquid foamed around it. She cleaned up the dried blood on his skin and applied another round of peroxide, satisfied when the foam stopped.

"I don't see any glass, but we need to check it again after the swelling goes down. *If* the swelling goes down," she corrected herself, cutting a piece of gauze that would fit perfectly over the wound. "Ty is gonna want to know what happened."

"And I'll tell him. No sense in keeping it from him. There's no way to hide the truck and he's not stupid."

Cecilia sat beside him, holding his hand. "I was listening to the scanner. I was so worried when you stopped answering. I didn't know what to do."

"I'd like to say I was perfectly safe. If I had been five seconds slower in turning around, we wouldn't be having this conversation right now."

She bit her bottom lip and looked into his eyes. "Was that the big one all the old timers said we were due for?"

Ryan shrugged. "I don't know. I thought I was pretty good about tracking these things, but then this happened, and it makes me realize I still have a lot to learn about weather. I want to say this was just a strong pattern that cleared out the atmosphere and we're good for a while, but now I'm going to second guess everything." He stood up and pulled his shirt over his head, tossing it into the hamper. "I need to check in with the department. I hope everyone got back safely."

"Me too, Ryan." His demeanor was unsettling. What exactly had he witnessed?

CHAPTER FOUR

Ryan's head throbbed and his shoulders ached. It was a little past midnight and insomnia had struck. Rolling on his side, he watched Cecilia as she slept, her breath shallow, her head buried in the pillow. Pulling the covers off, he padded to the bathroom, studying his reflection. The gauze was halfway off, and he peeled the rest of the tape back, tossing the soiled bandage in the trash.

The skin around the cut was beginning to bruise, and it pounded with the quickening of his pulse. Maybe Cecilia was right – he probably should have it looked at. The bleeding had stopped, but it looked nasty.

Grabbing a beer from the refrigerator, he stepped out on the back porch. It was chilly out, and he wished he would have grabbed a sweater. The air was damp and humid, but the sky was clear, revealing a bright blanket of stars. It was refreshing to see it. He loved intense weather and spring was his favorite season, but with the afternoon he had experienced, he would be happy if the rest of spring was calm and dry. He'd handle a drought if it meant not having to deal with storms like that again.

Sipping the beer, he finished it and tossed the bottle into the yard. Thinking about how lucky he had been, he felt his lips curl into a smile. Every man on the fire department with him had been accounted for, each one making it home safe and sound. There was no word on the storm chasers he had talked to, and there had been no mention of them on TV. No news was good news. It'd be all over the TV if someone was missing or had been killed.

When he closed his eyes, all he could see was the storm coming right at him. It was like it was alive, and the thunder was its loud growl, ready to devour him. The rotation was a black hole with one purpose – to suck him up and make him disappear. There were reports of people constantly going missing during tornadoes, and it was true – had those chasers not warned him about the shift in direction, he would be dead.

The whole time he was attempting to outrun it, he thought about Cecilia and Ty. They were his whole inspiration to keep going, to push the pickup past its limit. It was nothing short of a miracle that the vehicle had survived long enough to get him home, barely making it down the highway, crippled, limping, and on the verge of falling apart right in the middle of the road.

He wondered how long it'd take for him to not see the tornadic supercell every time he closed his eyes. Call it PTSD, call it being a wimp, call it whatever he wanted – he was not going to let it intimidate him. If the same thing happened tomorrow, he'd be ready to do his duty and protect his family. He'd go storm spot for the department if it meant getting people to safety before the storm came bearing down on them.

Walking toward the cellar, he lifted the door and went down the wobbly steps. The musty scent from before was even stronger, and he pulled the chain on the light, brightening the small hole in the ground. The bags of groceries they had bought earlier were in the same spot, and he went through each one, organizing them.

Maybe they wouldn't need to worry about it. Maybe this was the big one, as Cecilia had asked, and it'd be several more years before the weather cycled back.

Clutching a can of peaches, he peeled the label. "Mother Nature, you're a mean bitch."

He put the can back with the others. He closed the cellar and still wasn't tired, so he went to his truck, his heart sinking at the sight of it. They didn't have the money to get a new vehicle, and since he was storm chasing, insurance would never cover the damage. Working on cars was what he knew best, but the task of getting it drivable again seemed impossible.

He lifted the hood and with help from the full moon, he was able to get a good view of the engine. It wasn't in good shape, but the frame and bodywork were where the biggest challenge would be. Fidgeting with a few things, he ran his hands down the side of his shirt and closed the hood.

Sitting on the first step of the front porch, he looked up at the sky again. The brunt of the bad stuff was over. It *had* to be. Lightning never struck in the same place twice.

"I KINDA LIKE you giving me a ride to work." Ryan leaned over the console and kissed Cecilia. "It gives us a few more minutes together. Wanna meet for lunch?"

"I've gotta go to the school and eat with Ty. They're having some program where they want all the moms to come in. I think he brought the letter home about it last week. I promised him I'd do it."

Patting her thigh, he got out of the car. "I'll call you when I'm about done. Love you." He nodded toward Mrs. McElroy, but he couldn't get caught up chatting with her today. She'd probably have a lot to say about the storms, and by the looks of the garage, lots of people were lining up to get estimates on hail damage.

"Good morning, Ryan!"

"Morning, Mrs. McElroy. We'll come by here in a bit and get

some coffee!" Hoping she'd get the hint, he went inside and the waiting room of the shop was full of people.

"Ryan, we've got about twenty-five people who need repairs done." Justin handed him a clipboard. "Most have hail damage and shattered windows."

"I feel their pain," Ryan replied.

"Yeah, I saw the wifey drop you off. Your truck not so lucky?"

"The wifey is currently my bus ticket, yes." Ryan studied the list. "My truck is currently in bad shape, but I'll get her running again. With as busy as we are, I may never get to go home to do it." He motioned toward the cars taking up every bit of free space in the garage. "Is there anything we can fix fast? Something minor?"

"Define minor," Justin replied, his smile nervous.

"Something that won't take all damn day. We'll have to triage everything and prioritize it based on that."

"Triage?" Justin arched his eyebrow and took the clipboard from Ryan. The kid was a hard worker, but anything past spark plugs, engines, and brakes and he was clueless.

"Triage. You know, like what they do at hospitals. They see what is worse and what can wait to figure out where the hell to start."

"Ah!" Justin snapped his fingers. "Gotcha. Well, we've got a few cars with some minor dents. Then we've got some that were brought in on trailers."

Ryan went into the waiting room, trying to figure out what to do. There were only three certified mechanics on staff, including him.

"Ryan, how long do you think it'll take to fix my truck?" Several people asked the same questions, all of them speaking at once. Why were there so many people? He was the only mechanic shop in town, but Harper Springs didn't even get hit by the storm. Or maybe they had before it had shifted. Cecilia's car was okay, but they were ten miles outside of the city limits. It seemed like there was a narrow window where you either got hit hard, or you didn't get anything at all.

"If your car is currently drivable and safe on the road, I'm going to have to ask you to come back. We're at capacity for what we can work on, so please, if you're just here for some hail damage, you'll have to be put on a waiting list. I'll be more than happy to work on your cars, but right now I just can't get to them."

"How long do you think it'll take?"

Ryan couldn't pinpoint who asked the question, so he just directed the answer in the general vicinity of where the voice came from. "I'm not sure. Justin has taken your information down and we'll call you as soon as we can get you in. I'm going to get back there and start working on the vehicles that are in the worst shape, and then I'll have a ballpark figure of where we stand with the rest of you."

He didn't give anyone a chance to refute his decision and went to work on a truck that looked almost as bad as his. When he saw the name on the work order, he understood why – it was Chief Rayburn's, and he had been chasing the same night Ryan's truck had gotten demolished.

Rather than think about the past twenty-four hours, he dug into his work. Justin tackled another vehicle with the same caliber of damage, and the other mechanic didn't say a word when he came in, knowing the task at hand and getting down to it. With as complex as the vehicle damage was, they were in over their heads. He figured if he came in at six AM and worked twelve-hour days, he might be able to make a dent in them.

"Gibson, what's the verdict on my truck?"

Glancing over his shoulder, Ryan cleaned his hands off with a rag, but the oil was so thick that it was useless. Chief Rayburn stood at the entrance of the garage, his arms folded over his chest. Sometimes he was hard to read, coming off brash and hard, but sometimes he seemed to have a decent sense of humor.

CHAPTER FOUR

He joined Ryan, standing over the open hood. "It took in a lot of water, Chief. Might need a whole new engine."

His superior shook his head and clicked his tongue. "Shit. Probably worth more than the truck is. Can you get your hands on an engine?"

"I can try, but I'm not sure how long it'll take."

"Well, it's a Dodge. At least it's not foreign. And you're sure it needs a new one?"

Ryan straightened his posture and glanced at Justin. He worked fast and was finishing up a windshield on an old Chevrolet Cavalier. "I'm about ninety-five percent sure that it's the engine. Have you contacted your insurance company?"

Chief Rayburn raised his eyebrows and shifted his weight. "I have, but as you know, they won't cover it. They know damn well what I was out doing. It's no mystery. Damn, I should've never driven through that low spot off Roger's Dam. I probably floated for a good thirty seconds before the truck grounded itself again." He slammed his hand on the hood with a loud thud.

"I guess you can drive one of the department's trucks until we can get this fixed, but I wouldn't count on it happening for at least a week, maybe even longer." Ryan wiped his hands again. "My truck is in pretty bad shape too. I was able to get it home, but I don't think I can squeeze much more out of it. I'm not sure about Lieutenant Cannady. I think he stayed out of most of the severe stuff."

"Sounds like all of my men are out of commission except for him. Better hope we don't have to spot for a while. We'll have to depend on the sheriff's office, and some of those guys wouldn't know a tornado if it came down on top of them."

The mention of a tornado coming down on top of someone made the hair on the back of Ryan's neck stand up. It literally had happened to him, and he wouldn't wish it on anyone.

"Well, sir, I need to get back to work. As you can see, we're swamped with vehicles." He cringed at his choice of words. "I'll check on an engine for you and get you a quote on how much it'll cost."

"Thanks, Gibson."

Turning back to his work, Ryan had a hard time focusing. It was a shame they lived in a part of the country where they depended so much on their own transportation. Half the town was without a vehicle, and he was the only game in town to take care of them. At least Cecilia's car was okay. If it wasn't for that, he'd have no way to get to work. The town would have to revert to the old west days and travel by horse, and with the way things looked in his garage, it was a likely scenario.

Mrs. McElroy stopped by around lunch, dropping off sandwiches, coffee, and cookies for the guys. Ryan tried to give her some money for it, but she declined, stating that they were working hard for the people of Harper Springs, and it was on the house. It was a nice gesture, and it made him thankful for the small-town hospitality that most in the area still showed.

"You were right, Mrs. McElory," Ryan said between bites. "A big one hit. You know what you're talking about."

"We dodged a bullet here in town. It came close. Did your place get hit?"

"No ma'am. We were lucky too. You think we're up for anything else soon?"

She looked down at the floor, not answering him immediately. Maybe he shouldn't even have asked. "There's always that chance, Ryan. The air still feels different, but then again, I'm just a crazy old lady who never escaped this town." She laughed and patted him on the shoulder. "I'll leave you boys to it."

"Thanks for the sandwiches, Mrs. McElroy. If you ever need a tire rotation or a tune-up, it'll be on me."

"You're a sweet man, Ryan. They don't make them like you anymore." She winked and went back to her bakery. Ryan finished his sandwich and drank two cups of coffee, hoping it'd provide enough energy to get a few more cars done before it was quitting time.

CHAPTER FOUR

Cecilia called around five thirty and though he was ready to call it a day, Ryan wanted to finish up a few more things. He had let Justin and Marty head out, but he needed to fix what he could on Chief Rayburn's truck. It was more than a one-man job to pull the engine out, but he could at least do some body work. With minor pushback from his wife, mentioning his dinner getting cold and his son wanting to shoot some hoops, he was able to get off the phone and work until seven, when his body couldn't take much more. He had freed all the broken glass from the windshield and taken some of the side panels off.

Standing at the front of the garage, it was hard to believe he had worked almost twelve hours. By the looks of things, they hadn't done a damn thing, and Ryan tried hard not to get discouraged. They were three men. They could only do so much, and his customers would hopefully understand that.

Cecilia got to the garage around 7:15. She didn't look amused. "I saved you some dinner, but it probably won't be good leftover. Want to just stop and get a burger?"

"I'm sorry, babe. You should go inside and see the mess I'm having to deal with."

"Don't forget your truck. When are you gonna have time to finish it?"

Ryan shrugged. He was so tired that he couldn't think a rational thought, much less come up with a probable timeline for all of the shit on his to-do list. "A burger sounds fine." He reached into the back seat and nudged Ty. "Hey little man, how was school today?"

"Good. We had a tornado drill. We had to get in the hallway, kneel down, and put a book over our head."

"Yeah? That's good!"

"Does that mean we are going to have a tornado?" Ty's eyes widened and he gripped the Batman action figure in his small fingers.

Ryan glanced at Cecilia from the corner of his eye and back

to his son. "It's possible, kiddo. But probably not for a while, okay? Did you eat all your supper?"

"I did!"

"Then let's get you an ice cream cone. Sound good?" Thank goodness for Ty's short attention span. He didn't want to lie to the child, but he also didn't want to put scary ideas in his head.

Cecilia slipped her hand into Ryan's, her soft palm smooth against his oil-stained skin. "I'm sorry if I'm coming off bitchy. You work hard and everyone in Harper Springs appreciates it. Just don't overwork yourself. Do what you can do. That'll have to be okay with everyone, or too damn bad." She wrinkled her nose, but she couldn't come off mean even if she wanted to.

"I love you, Cecilia." Lifting her hand, he kissed the back of it.

"Love you too. Looks like a quiet night ahead of us. I know a good way we can pass the time if you're up for it." She wiggled her eyebrow, her flirtatious grin melting his heart.

"You know I'm always up for that."

A quiet night was exactly what they needed.

CHAPTER FIVE

The next day went smoothly for Ryan. The sun was out, and the temperatures were normal for that time of year. Even the news stations didn't mention much about any systems coming through, just an upper-level low that was going to keep most precipitation away. Ryan was prepared to work another twelve-hour day, and one of the biggest things on his to-do list was to find Chief Rayburn an engine for his Dodge.

Marty and Justin were there early with him, both already working on other vehicles. Ryan went into his office and did some research, finding the lowest-priced engine in a town about fifty miles away. Due to his current vehicle situation, the company was willing to deliver it for a fee. Ryan would eat the difference and not charge his chief with it, only agreeing to it for convenience.

Mrs. McElroy brought them more food, and this time, Ryan didn't take no for an answer when he tried to pay for everything. The day flew by, and Cecilia was waiting outside before he knew it. He knew better than to tell her to come back. He had some things he needed to take care of at home, and it finally felt like they were making some progress. Several people were able to pick up their cars and they were able to make a dent in the waiting list. Some people made snide comments about having to wait, but Ryan ignored them. Being out of routine made most people snarky and they'd eventually get over it as things slowly got back to normal.

Cecilia pecked him on the lips as he climbed into the passenger side. Ty held onto the same action figure he played with yesterday and was too busy making it fly around to pay attention to anything else.

"How was your day, hon?"

Ryan stretched his arms out and forced a smile. "Busy as hell. Yours?"

"I'm about halfway through making dinner. Figured you deserved a nice, home-cooked meal out on the patio. It's too beautiful to waste it inside."

Ryan nodded. "I hadn't really noticed. I was busy trying to find an engine for Chief Rayburn. Cheapest I could find was about twenty-five hundred dollars. And they're tacking on a hundred bucks for a delivery fee since I can't go pick it up."

"Is his truck worth that much?"

"Yeah, I guess. It's what he wants. The truck is only a couple of years old." Ryan yawned, fighting exhaustion. What he really wanted was an ice-cold beer and sleep. His body ached, and the wound on his forehead didn't look much better than the night he had gotten it. He was glad Cecilia hadn't mentioned it. It's not like she forgot it – the damn thing was noticeable with the purple bruising around the cut.

When they got home, Ryan went straight to the refrigerator and grabbed a beer. Though he was tired, he invited Ty out to shoot some hoops. The goal was lowered so that the boy could make a few. It was fun watching him learn the proper form, and though he was only five, he was a natural.

"Look, Daddy! I made it!" The ball swished through the net and Ryan passed it to him again. He struggled to catch it, but stuck with it and finally gained control.

"Good job! That was a great shot!"

CHAPTER FIVE

Cecilia came out on the porch, her hands on her hips. "Hey Ryan, I gotta run back into town. I forgot to pick up something, and supper will be a bust without it. One stupid ingredient! I knew I was forgetting something."

"Okay. We'll be good here. Pick up another twelve-pack, would you? I'm down to about three in there."

Cecilia smirked. "I guess so! Love you. Be back soon."

Ryan turned his attention back to Ty, who shot the ball again, only this time, it was an air ball. The boy pouted and curled his bottom lip. "I didn't make it!"

"That's okay, Ty. Even Michael Jordan missed sometimes."

"Michael Jordan?"

"The greatest athlete to ever play the game."

Ty dribbled the ball and passed it to Ryan. "I like Kobe Bryant. He's the best, Daddy!"

"Oh c'mon, don't even get started with who is the best, Ty!" He ruffled his son's hair, but the sudden shift in the wind caught his attention. The springlike air changed, and it was cold, much like the night he got caught in the storm. Ty passed him the ball again, but it hit his leg and bounced off the concrete court.

Walking to the edge of the yard, Ryan watched the sky over the mountains. It was the exact carbon copy of what he had witnessed, and his heart skipped a beat. This time, it was closer, with Harper Springs right in its path. Trees swirled and the clouds darkened. Small droplets of rain splattered like ice as it hit his skin.

Realizing he and Ty were still outside, he scooped his child up and ran into the house, turning the scanner and TV up. What the hell did he do with his phone? Rushing around the house, he found it on the nightstand in his bedroom.

"Daddy! What's wrong? Is there a tornado coming like we talked about in school?"

Ryan ignored him, attempting to get Cecilia on the phone. It rang several times, and she didn't answer. Redialing her, this time, a computerized voice came on, stating all circuits were busy. Shit! She shouldn't be out there!

He picked up Ty and took him everywhere he went, refusing to let him out of his sight. He needed to get hold of Cecilia somehow, so he rummaged through his truck, finding his radio in the floorboard.

Queuing the radio, he said, "This is Gibson. Anybody out there spotting?" The radio crackled and he thought he heard someone, but he couldn't tell what they said. "Who is that? Come in? Is there anyone out there?"

Trying one more time, he called her again, but it was the same story – all circuits were busy. Thunder echoed off the distant mountains, rumbling for what felt like hours. He went to the edge of the road, looking down the highway toward town. He didn't have much time. Maybe she was safely in a building with a basement, or maybe she realized what was happening and went to a neighbor's cellar.

Lightning flashed, knocking Ryan backward. It was close because the thunder was seconds later. Still clutching Ty, he shielded the boy as small pieces of hail fell from the rotating clouds. The cellar was close, and he forced his achy body to move quickly. He had to get Ty to safety – that was his main priority. With each step he ran, it was like the cellar was moving away from them, and the shards of hail were getting bigger, the lightning was closer, and the ice pelted him in the back, knocking the breath out of him. He hugged Ty close, shielding his son as best as he could.

Ty was crying and his death grip on Ryan's shirt was so tight that he could feel the fibers ripping in the fabric. Finally, he pulled the cellar door open, and the wind caught it, almost yanking it out of his hand.

"Get down inside, Ty! Hurry!"

Ryan went down the first few steps but paused when the tornado caught his eye. It was even bigger than the one that destroyed his truck and almost took his life, and it was in an adjacent pasture, coming right for them. High line wires sparked, the electrical poles dancing as the weather phenomenon pulled at them like they were toys. The suction was strong, ripping corn stalks from the ground and swirling them overhead. This time they wouldn't be so lucky, and though Ryan knew they were in immediate danger, he didn't move, watching like it was on TV and he was perfectly safe in his living room.

His neighbor's house a quarter mile away was ripped apart. He hoped they weren't home or were taking cover, but he couldn't remember if they even had a cellar. This was bad. Ryan was frozen, watching the world around him being destroyed by a mile-wide tornado that was growing by the second, feeding off the moist and dry air like a monster with an insatiable hunger.

"Daddy!"

Ty's screams pulled Ryan from his trance. It took every bit of his energy to get the door shut and secure. The cellar was pitch dark, and he pulled on the light switch. Surprisingly, they still had electricity, but it flickered, and it'd soon be out. He located the flashlights and lanterns, getting them ready for when they'd be left in the dark.

"Where's Mommy?" Ty began to cry, his eyes wide and full of fear.

Ryan's stomach lurched. She was out there somewhere, and he had to tell himself that she found cover. It came on so fast. The weather reports stated they'd be in a dry pattern, so this was catching everyone off guard.

"Where's Mommy?" Ty asked again, yanking on Ryan's pants.

"I don't know, Ty. I don't..." he lowered his voice. "I don't know." He had no other way to put it. What was he supposed to tell the kid?

Even though they were underground, everything shook like an earthquake. Debris pelted the cellar door, and it slammed up and down, the latches on the verge of giving way. If that happened, they'd be in trouble. The wind would serve as a vacuum and pull them right out into everything.

Backing Ty against the wall, Ryan stood between him and the door, keeping him as far away as possible, just in case the door ripped off and exposed them to the war zone above. He knew better than to go up the stairs and try and hold it in place. The sheer force of the storm would be no match, and he had to stay close to Ty.

"Daddy I'm scared!" The boy yelled, gripping Ryan's leg.

"It's gonna be okay." He said it to convince himself as well, though it wasn't working.

Everything was so loud that he couldn't even hear himself talk. The shelves in the cellar rattled, and a few of the groceries they had bought fell to the floor. Weren't tornadoes supposed to be quick and move on? What was going on outside? Maybe it just seemed longer than usual since they were in the middle of it.

As predicted, the door slammed a few more times, the hinges creaked, and the wind ripped it off like it was a piece of paper. Ryan grabbed Ty, holding onto him for dear life. Rain and hail hammered inside, but they were far enough back that it didn't hit them. He tried to find something to hold on to. If he didn't, the wind would pull them out. His body scooted toward the exit, his boots skidding across the dirt floor, but the walls of the cellar were helping, hindering the tornado from ripping them out of the cellar and into the sky.

Ryan had never felt anything like it. It was like he was weightless, and the helpless feeling was unnerving. Ty buried his face in Ryan's chest, and he pushed through the gale-force winds, crouching in the far corner, using the cabinets as a shelter from the hail and rain that was making its way inside.

"It'll be over soon, Ty." Comforting his son was impossible. He was terrified for Cecilia, wishing he could go back and stop her before she left for the grocery store. This was enough to scare anyone, and finally, the rain slowed, and the hail stones got smaller until they finally stopped. Getting to a standing position, Ryan looked up through the exit. The sky was still dark and swirling, but everything was calm. That wasn't necessarily a good thing, and he wasn't ready to get out and observe the damage. It wasn't over. The storm was still reeling, and he wished he could tell what the hell it was doing. It could easily backtrack like when he chased just a few nights before.

Turning to Ty, Ryan scooped him up and hugged him. The child was shaking, and he kissed the top of his head. How could he tell him to calm down when he couldn't even do it? Glancing up through the exit again, cloud-to-cloud lightning flashed and an instant rumble of thunder made Ryan scoot toward the back wall again.

"Is it over, Daddy?"

Ryan sat in the corner with Ty safely behind him. "I don't think so."

"Make it stop!" Tears fell down Ty's cheeks. "I want Mommy! Where's Mommy?"

"Everything is going to be okay."

Ryan had to keep telling himself that, not only to convince Ty but to convince himself. The storm re-organized and circled back around, throwing another round of severity over them. Without the cellar door protecting them, more hail was getting through, damaging whatever was in its path. Ryan tried to shield Ty and debris and hail hammered his back. Ty screamed over the loud rumble and when Ryan looked down at him, the boy's face was bleeding.

Unable to see where he was injured, Ryan held him, and hugged him close to his body, taking the brunt of the ice against his back. Ty was still conscious, but the blood was thick and streaming over his mouth. How in the world had he gotten hurt when Ryan had served as a shelter over him? Everything was happening so fast that he couldn't comprehend what was happening.

"Stay awake, Ty!" Ryan yelled as loud as he could, but he wasn't sure that Ty heard him. Closing his eyes, Ty let out a deep breath. "Stay awake!"

Things were happening quickly, but it felt like an eternity.

The first round of the storm lasted a long time, and the second round felt like 100 years had passed. Ryan was scared to leave Ty unattended, but he also wanted to try and get some idea of how much more of this they were in for. He held Ty, keeping his face against his chest. He was breathing but it was hard to tell if he was awake or not.

"Damn you!" Ryan yelled out, transferring his anger toward the sky. He was frustrated and scared, and rain pooled on the floor of the cellar, about an inch deep from the precipitation.

The storm stopped suddenly. Forcing himself to a standing position, he cradled Ty and looked at the sky. It was gray, but not as dark as it was before. Maybe the storm was finished and had moved on, or completely died off. That would have been the best-case scenario.

"Ty? Can you hear me?"

The child's eyes fluttered open for a second and he moaned. "Dad?"

Reaching for a flashlight, Ryan dug through their supplies and came across a first aid kit. He cleaned Ty's face as best as he could, finding the injury on Ty's temple. It was deep and he could see tissue. He needed medical attention. There was a bottle of ibuprofen, and he shook one out and grabbed a bottle of water.

"I know you don't like taking pills, but can you do this for me? It'll help your head. Does your head hurt?"

Ty's eyes were open, but only halfway, like he was on the verge of sleeping. He needed to stay awake in case he had a concussion. He nodded and cringed. Opening his mouth, Ryan slipped the pill in and let the boy drink as much as he needed. He struggled at first, spitting it out, and Ryan tried to be patient. He had never been good at taking medicine, and though the pill was small, he gagged. Finally, after the third try, it went down.

"Help will be here soon, and we'll get you to a doctor."

"My arm hurts too."

Ryan pulled out a camping chair from their supplies and laid

CHAPTER FIVE

it flat where Ty would have a spot to spread out. His arm was limp and that's when Ryan got his first glimpse of a small piece of bone protruding just below Ty's elbow. How in the hell did that happen? He thought he had taken the brunt of the hail and debris coming in.

"Don't move it, Ty. Let me see if I can find something to splint it with."

He felt guilty and worried. What if there were more injuries he didn't know about? What if something internal was going on? He dug through the first aid kit, but it was nothing but a basic box with band-aids, ointment, and a few gauze pads. That wouldn't help.

Pulling his phone from his pocket, he cursed when he saw there was no signal available. Maybe if he got out of the cellar, it'd be a different story. It would also give him a chance to see what the weather was doing. He wouldn't stray too far away and get separated from Ty. He'd be right there, ready to jump back down if something happened.

Kneeling beside the lawn chair, Ryan ran his hand through Ty's hair. He had to be in so much pain, but any more than one ibuprofen for a boy his size was a bad idea. He'd have to rotate it with Tylenol and keep track of the time for future doses. The pain medicine probably wasn't even making a dent in what he was going through.

"Ty, I'm going to go up to ground level and see if I can get my phone to work. I'm not going to go far, I promise. Do you need anything before I go up there?"

Ty opened his eyes again and they fluttered like it was taking every ounce of energy he had. "I want Mommy," the boy whispered. "I hurt, Daddy. My arm..." he closed his eyes again.

"Try and stay awake, Son. I'll be right back."

A lump formed in Ryan's throat. How could he have let this happen? First, Cecilia was out there in it and now his son was in bad shape. He had to do something, and fast.

The stairs were torn to pieces, leaving only a few safe enough to use. Ryan had to climb his way up the wall, using the wall for leverage to get to the top. Ty wouldn't be able to make that climb when it was time to get him out. When he crawled out of the cellar, he got his first glance at the damage - it took his breath away.

CHAPTER SIX

Their house was gone. The only evidence that a home had ever been there was the concrete foundation and what was left of the trees that surrounded it. Most of the branches were gone, leaving only stumps to prove that people once inhabited the land. Ryan turned in a circle, desperately attempting to control his panic. The barn was also gone, and his truck was nowhere to be found.

There were no signs of human life anywhere – no cars on the highway, no houses for miles where homesteads once were. There were no cattle or farm animals. Whatever had come through had completely stripped the land, leaving nothing behind.

A hazy gray sky blanketed over him. Where was the sun, and would they ever see it again?

Ryan pulled his phone from his pocket,. Still no signal, but he went ahead and tried to dial out. How bombarded would 911 be? Emergency workers were probably being pulled in every direction, causing long wait times.

"We're sorry. All circuits are busy. Please hang up, and try again later." The tinny computer voice was like a punch to the gut, and Ryan tried again, receiving the same message several times.

He also tried Cecilia's number, but the phone wouldn't dial out. He only had about fifty percent battery life left, so he turned it off to preserve energy. There was no sense in keeping it on if the signal was shot and 911 was unavailable.

Since there was no telling when help would come, Ryan searched for something he could make a splint out of. With tree branches scattered all over the place, he had several choices. He needed a flat piece, and one he could easily break since Ty was so tiny. He gathered up several pieces and took them down into the cellar. Splashing through the pool of water on the floor, he stopped at the foot of the lawn chair that Ty was laying on.

"Ty?" His eyes were closed, but when Ryan called his name, he tried to sit up.

"Dad?"

"No, don't get up. Just keep trying to stay awake."

"Why do I have to stay awake? I want to sleep. I'm sleepy."

Ryan put the wood down beside the first aid kit and took his shirt off. He had a white tank top on underneath, so he could use one to make a sling.

"I just need you to stay awake. I might need your help, okay?" He didn't want to go into full detail about the possibility of a concussion, nor would Ty understand it anyway.

"Okay."

Ryan could tell he was not feeling well because he was usually full of questions about everything. Ryan tried not to overthink the situation. No cell phone signal, no other signs of people around, and their house was gone. They were pretty much stranded with no timeline on when this might be over. And he also hated not knowing what the weather was going to do. If another storm barreled through, they might not be so lucky. The cellar already had standing water in it. What if it rained hard enough to drown them?

Steadying a slab of wood, he measured it against Ty and was able to break it about the length of his forearm.

CHAPTER SIX

"This might hurt a little, Ty, but it'll help you not move it around."

Ryan put the wood in place and tied it with strips of gauze. Lifting his shirt, he tried to figure out a good way to tie it to make a sling. Slipping Ty's arm in it, it wasn't the prettiest concoction, but at least it took some pressure off the injury and maybe Ty could get a break from the pain. Ryan applied some ointment around the bone sticking out, being careful not to put too much pressure on it. The last thing they needed was for it to get infected. He also checked the wound on Ty's temple, keeping it covered. It had stopped bleeding, but it still looked ugly.

What was most surprising was how calm Ty was. Maybe his body was in shock, and he was numb to it. Though shock was a scary thing, at least he wasn't hurting. That also meant he'd need to get medical attention faster. Ryan had to keep talking to him. He couldn't let him sleep until he knew more about his injuries.

Ryan was second-guessing himself. He had no experience in the medical field. What if Ty needed sleep so his body could heal? He had experience with the fire department, but it didn't go past basic first aid. They had real paramedics who hopped in and did the dirty work. He just fought the fires and got people to safety.

Pulling out another lawn chair, he sat beside Ty and tried not to panic. They had a decent supply of food, and he silently thanked Cecilia's father for urging them to go stock up – Ryan just wished they would've gotten more. If he rationed the food and gave most of it to Ty for strength, they were good for at least a week, if not more. Hopefully, they'd be out of there by then, but it was hard to say. He'd never encountered something like this. The storms he had been in before were brief and crippling, but help was there in no time.

He estimated that an hour had passed, and there were still no signs of other life around them. Whatever had happened, or however big it was, it had completely debilitated everyone for miles. Would it be better to stay put and wait, or go find someone? He also wondered about his father – he lived on a small farm nearby, but his cellar wasn't safe and halfway caved in. Ryan had offered to go fix it, but his father always refused the help. Was he able to take cover and survive?

Ryan didn't know what to do – Cecilia wasn't there, Ty was hurt, and the well-being of his father was up in the air, not to mention Cecilia's parents. They were well prepared, but did they have enough warning? The system came on fast. So many people were probably caught off guard and left for dead.

Unable to sit still for too long, Ryan rummaged through their camping supplies. He came across two wool blankets he had stuck in there before their last excursion in the mountains, and he draped one around Ty. Keeping his body temperature regulated might help with shock, as well as add some comfort for him.

With his free arm, Ty pulled it up around him and a small smile parted his lips, though the expression didn't last long.

"You feeling okay, buddy?" Ty didn't answer and let out a sigh. Leaning over him, Ryan kissed his head. "You hungry?"

"A little."

That was a good sign. Ryan was hungry too, and a sign of an appetite made him feel a little better. He opened a can of Vienna sausages and a package of saltine crackers and handed Ty one of each. He scarfed them down and Ryan gave him more. He was never a fan of canned meat, but they tasted pretty good. He was only able to stomach a couple and gave the rest to Ty, along with more water. Checking his watch, he shook out one Tylenol from the bottle in the first aid kit.

"Can you be a big guy and swallow another pill for me?"

Ty hesitated at first, holding the water bottle up to his lips. "Okay."

Slipping the pill in his mouth, it went down easier than the ibuprofen from earlier.

"Are you hurting anywhere?" Ryan asked, feeling like he should be wearing a white coat and carrying around a clipboard.

"My arm feels like my heartbeat is in it."

"It's throbbing?"

Ty's brow furrowed. "Throbbing? What's that?"

Ryan laughed. "It's like when it feels like your heartbeat is there," repeating the young child's take on the injury. "Tell me if it starts to hurt really bad, okay?" He put the medicine back in the first aid kit.

"Where are you going, Daddy?"

"I've gotta figure out how to fix the steps in here. The storm tore them all to sh..." He stopped himself from cursing. "The storm tore them up, and it'll be hard for you to get out of here with a broken arm. But don't worry. I'll figure something out."

"Are you leaving me here?"

"No. If I go up there," Ryan pointed up to the exit that was now just a hole in the ground, "I'll be right within earshot, so if you need me for anything, just call for me. I promise I'll be right here. I'm not going anywhere."

Climbing back up to the war zone, he tried to figure out what he could build that would be good enough to get Ty out of there. With no idea what the weather was going to do, he wasn't in a rush to bring him up, and with their food supply, they were doing okay. If anything, he could make a ladder and hoist him up with one arm.

He gathered up any strong pieces of wood he could find. There was debris everywhere, but most of the branches from trees were too fragile to support his weight if he made it into a ladder. He went ahead and piled up that wood too so he could start a fire if needed. Pausing, he stretched and looked up at the sky. It was dark again, and the sun never made an appearance after the storm. It was almost eight PM and he was about to lose any chance of natural light, and that was unsettling. If another storm was brewing, he wouldn't be able to see what was coming.

He was tired both physically and mentally, and his shoulders ached as he carried the wood to a small pile next to the entrance of the cellar. He needed to check on Ty, so he slipped down the cellar wall, kneeling beside his son.

"Ty?"

The boy's eyes flickered open. "Dad. Am I at the hospital? Did you get me out?"

"No. We're still in the cellar, Son, but you're safe. How are you feeling?"

"My arm is..." he stopped, looking around. "What's that word you said about a heartbeat?"

Ryan smiled. "Throbbing?"

"Yeah, it's throbbing."

"Are you hungry?"

Ty shook his head no. The flashlight wasn't lighting up the cellar well, and he wanted to preserve the batteries, so he pulled out two lanterns and hooked up propane to each of them. Thankfully, the matches were in a plastic box and had been protected from the rain, and he lit each one, making the room bright like they had electricity.

Sifting through their food, he saw the can of tamales and his heart sank. He thought about his conversation with Cecilia at the grocery store. She was right – if he got hungry enough, he'd eat them, but he wasn't to that point yet. They had only been in the cellar for a few hours, but he definitely could eat. Another can of Vienna sausages would have to do. He was too tired to pull the camp stove out and he didn't want to eat up everything. By the way things looked, they could be there a while.

He offered Ty one of the sausages, but he declined. His lack of appetite was concerning. At least he was staying hydrated. The cellar was a blessing, but one thing Ryan hated was not being able to see what the weather was doing. The small hole where the door once was only gave him a small preview of the sky and not even the stars were showing. The cloud cover might have been a good thing – sometimes that meant that severe weather wouldn't be able to form until the cap burned off.

He walked up the undamaged steps, seeing if he could get a

CHAPTER SIX   51

better glimpse at a different angle, but he stopped in his tracks. Was he hearing voices? Did someone finally come to help? Climbing up the wall, he scooted through the exit and saw two men coming down his driveway. He didn't recognize them, and they didn't look like they were involved with emergency services. Maybe they had to send in reinforcements from surrounding towns since everything there was crippled.

"How's it going over here?" One of the men spoke up, his hair disheveled, his face caked with dirt and mud.

"Good. Are you with FEMA or emergency services?"

The man looked at his friend and laughed. "Do I look like I'm with FEMA?"

Ryan shrugged, his instincts suddenly screaming at him that these guys were up to no good. Guarding the cellar, he kept an eye on each of them. How was it already getting to this? There were already looters roaming the area? Maybe he was jumping to conclusions too fast.

"Well, can I help you with anything?"

The other guy spoke up. "You got any food down there?"

Ryan didn't want to turn them away. If the situation were reversed and he needed help, he'd hope other people would be hospitable. But he couldn't give up much. They didn't have a whole lot to spare.

"A little. You've been walking around, yeah? How does everything look?"

"Terrible. You're the first person we've found, and we've stopped at several farms. Either people are staying in their cellars, or they got blown away with their houses. What kind of food do you have?" The man ran his hands together, his smile making the hair on the back of Ryan's neck stand up.

"Can I ask you something?" Ryan asked. "Did you see a car down the highway by chance? A silver Toyota? I'm not sure how close to town it would've gotten, but did you see one?"

"I don't think you understand how serious this situation is, mister. Everything from here to Fox Lake and God knows how far has been wiped off the map. If you weren't below ground when the shit came through, you're probably dead. Whoever was driving this silver Toyota that you speak of is probably dead." The man paused, his smile widening, exposing yellowed teeth. "It was your lady, wasn't it?"

"I'm gonna grab you two a little food. I'll be right back."

Ryan didn't want to let them get out of sight, but he also wanted them off his property. Maybe if he gave them what they wanted, even if it wasn't much, they'd move on. He grabbed a couple of cans of potted meat and stopped before going back to ground level. Ty was safely in the far corner, oblivious to what was happening above them. He remembered the nine-millimeter Glock he kept in one of the cabinets. He had put it there a few months back after purchasing it in hopes to keep it out of reach of Ty. And now, it served a purpose.

Putting it in the waistband of his jeans, he adjusted his shirt to hide it. He went back up and extended the cans to them, each scoffing as they snatched them away.

"Potted meat? You gotta be kidding me. I know you got more shit down there. A guy like you probably stocked up like all those jackasses in line at the grocery store. What else you got?"

"That's about it." Ryan felt the heavy gun on his hip, its weight a reminder that he wasn't going to let these guys push him around.

"Bullshit." One of the men stepped forward, but Ryan stood his ground, not moving away from the cellar entrance. "You believe this guy? Thinks he can take on both of us?" Getting in Ryan's face, he could smell the man's stale breath. "Step aside. I'm going down there to see what else you have."

Ryan didn't move. How could it already get to this point? Was it as bad as they were claiming, or were they just seeing an opportunity to rob people?

"Take what I gave you and go. My son is injured, and the rest of the food is to keep him healthy until help comes."

"I got news for you. Ain't no help coming. Keep telling yourself that, but it's like the end of the world out there. I already told you that you're the first person we've talked to for miles. No one is coming."

"Well, you'll have to go loot someone else because I'm not giving you anything else."

"He's a brave man, ain't he!" The man turned to his friend, and that's when Ryan took the chance to grab the gun from his pants. Holding it out, he pointed it at the stranger, gripping the handle so tight that his knuckles ached. He was trained on how to shoot and handle a gun, but he never had to point it at a human being.

"Woah, look at this! He's even got a gun! Go figure, in Texas of all places!" The sarcasm in the man's voice was thick, but he was nervous, despite trying to hide it.

"I need you to leave, right now." Ryan's voice shook and he took a step closer.

"You don't have the sack to pull the trigger."

Ryan raised it in the air and fired one, keeping in mind the minimal supply of ammunition he had. It echoed in the dense air. "The next one will be between your eyes if you don't start marching back that way." He pointed the gun toward the road. When it came to his son's protection, he was willing to do it.

The men took a second, not wanting to show their weakness, but they did as told, taking their time. "We'll be back. And you better hope we don't find that silver Toyota you were asking about."

Ryan clenched his jaw and kept the gun trained on them until they were out of sight. If the thieves and looters were already coming out, he'd have to secure the cellar. He didn't want to believe that people were already resorting to violence, but in desperate times, people either worked together to make it or they split up and instantly went into survival mode.

With the cellar door gone, he'd have to rig up something that protected them. Fixing the steps would have to wait.

CHAPTER SEVEN

Darryl Gibson was surprised he made it through the storm. The only thing remaining of his house was his wraparound porch, and he narrowly missed the tornado and hail by a few seconds. Climbing from his cellar, he noted the time on his watch – it was a little after six in the morning and there was still no sign of the sun. The cloudy sky lent an ominous view, and it was as dark as night. He was shocked when he finally got the first view of all the damage around his place.

Stepping onto the porch, the wood was weak under his boots, bowing with his weight. Several trees remained standing, but the branches were torn up so badly that it'd take a long time to get them back the way they were. He also surveyed all the uprooted trees – the tornado had unscrewed them like a cork from a wine bottle.

He rarely carried his cell phone with him, but pulled it from his pocket, thankful he had it on him. He wasn't the best at using it, but he searched through his recent calls and tried to dial Ryan, but nothing happened. It didn't ring and the screen displayed *"call dropped"*, flashing in bold letters. He worried about Ryan – he had Cecilia and Ty to care for, and hopefully, he was able to get them to safety in time. They had a nice cellar, much better than his that was halfway caved in. It was nothing short of a miracle that it had protected him, and it probably wouldn't be able to handle another storm without the chance of it completely collapsing and burying him alive.

There was also no sign of his horses. He owned ten and they were nowhere to be found. Where were the fire department and ambulances? His closest neighbors were about half a mile down the road, so he couldn't tell if they had made it to safety before the storm came through.

Darryl had been through some big storms, but never one that took his house. He had to get to Ryan and check on them. Along with his house, his farm truck was gone. He ran his boot over the oil stain on the gravel driveway where he parked, the only evidence that he even owned a vehicle. With no horses and no vehicle, the trip would take a while. He lived south of Harper Springs and Darryl was north, and he estimated that on foot, it would take about half a day, and that was in good conditions. There was no telling how the highways and roads would be with downed power lines and trees blocking the way.

He tried calling his son again, with the same result. The cell phone signal was shot, and he resisted the urge to break the phone in half. Eventually, it'd serve a purpose again, once things got back to normal, so he slipped it back into his pocket and turned his anger to something else. Kicking a rock as hard as he could, it flew and hit a tree stump a few yards away. How in the hell could this have happened? He had to keep a calm head and think about his next steps – getting to Ryan, Cecilia, and his grandson was important, and along the way, he could check on neighbors.

The silence was so loud – where was everyone, and what would they do if another storm came through?

He needed a horse. With no signs of human life anywhere, what were the chances of finding one? They were smarter when it came to weather. That's how Darryl usually knew the bad stuff was coming – he'd just watch the pasture, and if the horses were acting strange, it was a good indication they were in for something. But this time, it had caught everyone off guard. Did that include the livestock?

He walked toward the back pasture where he kept them. Only a few pieces of wood stuck out of the ground where the barn had been. There was no wildlife, cows, horses, or anything. A worried feeling settled in the pit of his stomach. He was concerned for everyone, but especially his son and family. It had been over a week since he had spoken to Ryan, and he regretted that even though they lived close to each other, they rarely got together.

He had no supplies or food. There was a faucet that had survived only because the plumbing was deep in the ground, and he cupped his hands, sipping water before it dribbled between his fingers. Patting his face, he washed the dirt and grit on his skin, and it felt rejuvenating. He needed to find something to put water in, especially if he was going to walk toward Ryan's place. With the weather changes, there was a chance he could run into every anomaly possible. Extreme heat, more severe thunderstorms, and even snow. He couldn't take it lightly, especially since they were transitioning from winter to spring.

Maybe the worst was over. Maybe the atmosphere was cleared out and the sun would show. For now, it was dark and ominous, and he needed a horse and canteen. He had to get moving, for the sake of his livelihood and for his son's family. They needed to stick together and each second that passed was precious.

His next big decision was whether he needed to continue to look for a horse, or if he needed to channel his energy toward walking. His horses were good about staying close to the house, and with no sign of them in the field, the chances of them showing back up were slim.

Going back into the cellar, he steadied himself. The hole was compromised before the weather, so he had to be careful that it didn't finish caving in. He had moved most of his supplies out and to the barn, but he rummaged just in case – maybe he left something behind that would hold water.

In a far cabinet, buried under a mound of dirt, he found a canteen. He was so thrilled that he yelled out in joy. He knew he had one somewhere, and there it was! It was almost too convenient, but Darryl wasn't going to question the circumstance. Pulling it out, he dusted it off on his jeans, and several dirt clods fell from the ceiling.

The cellar shook like an earthquake, the weak wooden beams moaning from the force of the dirt surrounding it. Darryl was frozen for a second, watching streams of dirt and mud shoot from above, and finally, he got his feet to move. Sprinting to the steps, he took them up to ground level, moving faster than he ever had. The earth imploded with each step he took, seconds away from swallowing him inside the destroyed cellar.

When he was back on solid ground, he turned to look at the destruction. The cellar was nothing more than a large hole, dust floating upward. He had barely shifted the mound of dirt on the inside, and it caused a collapse. He was lucky the tornado hadn't finished the job with him inside, completely helpless with nowhere to go.

Clutching the canteen, he wiped the sweat from his brow and ambled over to the faucet. Rinsing it clean, he filled it up and drank almost half, his parched lips craving every drop he brought to it. He refilled it and told himself he had to ration it. On foot, the journey to Ryan's house was going to be a challenge. As long as he stayed hydrated and didn't run out of water, he could do it. He *had* to do it. There was no other choice.

RYAN DIDN'T SLEEP A WINK. He worried about Ty and about the looters, and with the makeshift piece of metal he had found in a field serving as their only security, he wasn't able to sit still. He continued to check Ty – with head injuries, sleeping could be bad thing, especially if he had a concussion. He seemed comfortable and didn't complain about pain. That could also be his body in shock, which meant the longer he was without medical attention, the worse everything would get.

He pulled out some instant coffee and measured out a couple of spoonful's, stirring it in a plastic cup. He didn't take the time to heat water – it was lukewarm, and while it wasn't the best, it aided in appeasing his caffeine addiction.

Kneeling beside Ty, he watched him for a few seconds. His son was still asleep, and for the first time since the tornado, he looked comfortable. Ryan told himself it was a good thing – he couldn't harp on the possibility of it being detrimental to his health.

He pulled out a jar of peanut butter. It'd be a good, filling breakfast that wouldn't take too much out of their surplus. Using the same spoon he stirred the coffee with, he ate a glob and took a sip of coffee. He adjusted the lantern, brightening the cellar. With the piece of metal over the exit, it had made the room pitch black, and he was curious to see what the weather was like outside.

Finishing his coffee, he climbed up the wall and slid the homemade door open. It was cloudy and humid, but the heat hadn't set in. There was still no sign of the sun, and Ryan was starting to miss it. No wonder people up north got depressed during winter – with no sun, it affected his mood. Or maybe it was the whole situation – he needed to talk to Cecilia, her parents, and his father. He needed to make sure they were all okay and accounted for.

He kept the pistol in his pocket. What if those guys came back with their weapons? He had to be ready. It was a shame people resorted to that kind of behavior in emergencies, instead of pulling together and helping each other. He would've been glad to give them more food, but when they threatened him and his son, Ryan's protective instincts came out.

He needed to find a way to lock the cellar. With the barn half gone and all his tools missing, it was going to be a challenge. He kept the sturdy wood separate – his plan with that pile was to rebuild the steps that had been torn to shit. At least he still had the Swiss Army knife in his pocket. He never went anywhere without it, and it'd serve a crucial role in his attempt to rebuild their bunker.

Grabbing the thin branches that were scattered over the ground, he cut strips off them, keeping the pieces as long as possible. Weaving them in and out of each other, he made as many pieces of rope as he could. He braided them, his fingers raw as he tightened the strips. If he couldn't rebuild the stairs, he could make a stretcher for Ty to get him out that way.

"Dad?"

Ty's voice echoed below, and Ryan shimmied down to meet him. "Hey, Ty. How are you feeling?"

"I'm hungry. What time is it?" He was groggy and rolled on his side, keeping the weight off his arm.

Ryan glanced at his watch. "Seven in the morning. Want me to make you some breakfast?" Maybe Ty should get up and walk. He wasn't a medical expert, so every decision he made regarding his son had him second-guessing himself.

"Yeah. What do we have?" Ty sat up, his dark hair disheveled.

"How about you come over here and help me look through everything?" Ryan motioned toward the cabinet full of food.

Ty hesitated but swung his legs over the side of the lawn chair and got to his feet, taking a second to gain his composure. He moved forward, taking it slow. Meeting him at the counter, he grabbed one of the bags with his good arm.

"Is that oatmeal?" Ty held up a tan package and shook it.

"Instant oatmeal. Is that what you want?"

"We don't have a microwave, Dad."

"No, but I can fire up the camp stove."

Ty nodded and sat down on the lawn chair as if the small walk to the food had taken everything out of him. "Where's Mommy? How come she's not here?"

Ryan felt a lump form in his throat. Connecting a bottle of propane to the stove, he struck a match and lit the front burner. The orange and blue flames were small, but they'd do the trick in warming up water for the oatmeal. He had been trying to find a way to explain the situation to Ty, but he couldn't think up the words. The truth was the best thing, even if his son was only five years old.

He stirred the oatmeal into the water and looked at Ty. "She went to the store to get something for supper. And that's when the storm hit, Ty. I don't..." Ryan looked down at the stove and back up. "I'm not sure where she is."

"Did the tornado get her?" Ty's eyes were red and swollen, maybe from exhaustion, maybe from sadness. It was hard to tell.

"No, Ty. I don't think the tornado got her." Ryan hoped to God he was right. He poured the oatmeal into a plastic cup and handed it to him. "Let me get you a spoon."

Ty ate like it was a delicacy, slurping up every bit. "Can you call her?"

Ryan pulled his cell phone out and turned it on. No signal, no missed calls, or messages – his battery life was holding strong, but once it was dead, that was it. "I tried before, but I can try again. I'll have to do it up there." He pointed upward. "I'm going to find her, Ty. I promise you, I'll find her."

He was in a predicament. He couldn't leave his kid to go look for Cecilia, and Ty was in no shape to run all over the area in search of his mother. He was showing signs of slow improvement, but it would deteriorate if he didn't get adequate rest. His arm wouldn't heal until he had surgery – moving him around could make it worse. And the longer Ryan waited, the chances of locating Cecilia grew slimmer. He also didn't want to leave their food supply behind. It'd surely be gone by the time they got back, and they also had a stable structure to protect them in case more severe weather came through. He couldn't put Ty in danger. He couldn't let anything else happen to him.

CHAPTER SEVEN

"I'm gonna climb up there really quick and see if I can call her, Ty. Drink your water. All of it."

At ground level, he balled his fists and cursed at the sky. He needed something to work out. He needed answers to all the questions! His worry for Cecilia had been constant on his mind, but this was the first time he felt on the verge of losing his cool. Warmth escaped the corners of his eyes, and the moisture trailed down his cheeks. Swiping the tears with the back of his hand, he paced near the pile of rope he had constructed.

When he dialed her number, there was no response. It ate away about two percent of his battery, so he quickly shut it off. It was a dead end, but he had to try, especially since Ty had requested it. He sat down and hugged his knees to his chest, looking up at the sky. How in the hell could this have happened? How come no one was coming to help? Where were Red Cross and FEMA? It was like they were shut off from the entire world.

What was he going to do? He had to find Cecilia, but he also had to protect his son. Someone had to come for them soon. Maybe Cecilia was safe at a hospital or a shelter in town and they'd be reunited soon. It was Ryan's desperate attempt to be positive, and he had to hold onto the small bit of hope to stay strong for Ty. If he lost his cool now, they didn't stand a chance.

CHAPTER EIGHT

Darryl checked his watch. He had only been walking a little over an hour and he felt like he had barely gotten anywhere. The temperature was growing as the sun started to come out, and walking on the asphalt made it seem even hotter. He was happy to see the sun, and it was good and bad – with the heat rising, it meant storms could organize due to daytime heating. He'd guess that it was at least 95 degrees, and it wasn't even nine AM yet.

What if they had record-breaking heat to accompany the severe storms? What would stop it from going from one extreme to the other, from nasty tornadoes to a blazing inferno that would bake everyone?

He adjusted his baseball cap and swiped the hair from his forehead. It was plastered to his skin, and when he licked his lips, it felt like sandpaper. He was afraid to drink too much water. All he had on him was the canteen, and the more he opened it, the warmer it'd get. The Fox River that fed into Fox Lake was coming up in a few miles. He could refill then, but with all the damage and debris, the sanitation of the water would possibly be compromised.

Shaking his head, he laughed to himself. He had looked at

some water purification tablets at a camping store not long ago and wondered what the hell he'd do with something like that. The irony of the situation was so bad that Darryl fought the urge to cry. On a normal day, no one would ever think to buy a package. Now, it was a necessity he thought he'd never need.

Not a single car had come down the highway, which lent an eerie feel to Darryl's surroundings. It wasn't a busy interstate, but cars came and went at all hours of the day. He'd passed by a few abandoned ones, and with no one around, he searched each one, hoping to find anything that might help him, but came up short.

A small rain shower would be great. Nothing severe, just enough to knock the temperature down and cool him off. Instead, the sun beat down on him, making him feel like he was in hell.

He saw another abandoned car about 200 yards ahead. Quickening his pace, he fought his aching body. It was a Toyota, much like what Cecilia drove. His heart sank. Was this her car? It looked a lot like it, and when he saw the booster seat in the back, it confirmed it was. There was no sign of her or Ty. Where were they going? Was Ryan with them, and if so, why did they take the car and not his truck, which would be sturdier?

Opening the door, he reached for the keys, but they were gone too. He searched the console and under each visor, and an insurance card fell onto the seat. Skimming it, he saw Ryan and her name as primary drivers, and the sense of dread heightened.

Were people just vanishing into thin air? The fact that the car was in one piece made him feel better. It meant that they didn't get tossed inside, but stranger things could happen. Tornadoes were known for skipping one house and then demolishing the next.

Darryl ran out into the field, yelling out each of their names. The trees swayed in the breeze, and no one answered back. It was the first time he noticed there weren't any birds flying or chirping like they usually did on an early spring morning. Life as he knew it was gone, and he felt like the only man left on a planet that was destroying itself.

"Ryan!"

He ran into the field, hoping they were hiding somewhere, taking cover outside of the car, but there was nothing. No footprints, nothing ever giving a hint that they were there – only Cecilia's car, abandoned, leaving no trace of anything behind.

When Darryl calmed down, he figured out he was on Farmer Johnson's land. Due north of the mileage marker was where his house once stood, so he hurried in that direction. Maybe they had gotten into his cellar and were just waiting for help.

Just as he expected, the house was gone. The foundation was still there, but to the left was a closed cellar door. Flinging it open, he looked inside, but it was dark.

"Ryan? Cecilia?"

His voice echoed and no one responded. He felt a tap on his shoulder, and he turned on his heel, gasping. Two men were behind him. He didn't recognize either of them.

"Can we help you, mister?"

"I'm looking for Farmer Johnson. Where is he?" The men struck him wrong, and he backed away to keep a safe distance.

"Not here, as you can see." One man nudged the other and they laughed.

"Where is he?" He thought about asking if they had seen his family, but he kept that detail to himself until he got a better idea of who the strangers were.

"He didn't make it. Neither did his wife."

"How do you know? Did you find their bodies?"

"I guess you could say that."

One of the men flashed a light down into the cellar, revealing a bloody blanket in the corner. Darryl's pulse raced and he took another step back in case he needed to run. It couldn't be. He had just talked to Johnson a few days ago about buying a horse from him.

"You didn't…"

CHAPTER EIGHT

"We needed food. Desperate times call for desperate measures. You know the old saying."

Darryl bit his bottom lip. "The police will get you for this. They were good people." His voice shook and he tried to hide his emotion.

"The police aren't coming, old man. Can't you see? We're all on our own now. Fend for ourselves. Survival of the fittest. It's like the end of the world, and I'm not going to let me or my brother suffer. Take charge now!" He scrubbed his hand down the back of his neck. "You got anything we can use?"

"No." The canteen was heavy on his hip, but maybe they wouldn't see it under his shirt.

"Then you are no use for us, just like the Johnsons weren't."

He pulled a knife out, and Darryl backpedaled and turned to run. There was no indication that they had a gun or weapon, and he cursed himself for leaving all his in his house. They were gone like everything else, but he never figured he'd run into something like that. It was like he was stuck in an end-of-the-world movie with criminals and looters.

No gunshots rang out. No one came after him. Maybe they'd stay close to their food supply and leave him alone. When he finally felt safe enough to, his pace slowed to a walk, and he glanced over his shoulder. The poor Johnsons probably invited them right down for food, and they turned on them. Was the situation really that bad? With the absence of emergency personnel, it was plausible. People panicked and slipped into survival mode when routines and ways of life were interrupted by disaster.

There were so many questions on Darryl's mind. Why was Cecilia's car abandoned on the side of the highway? Who was with her? Or even worse – had the two thieves and murderers already been to Ryan's house? Was Ryan, Ty, and Cecilia dead like the Johnsons?

He had to get to his son's place. Time was against him, and he needed to make sure they were okay. He'd only stop for water and to take short breaks. If he kept up the pace, maybe he'd make it by the time the sun went down, as long as no other issues came up.

RYAN MADE several strands of rope, pulling them as tight as he could. With too much weight, they'd snap – the wood was already starting to get dry, and he wondered if Ty would be too heavy. He counted the good pieces of wood he planned to make steps out of. There were only a few that would prove useful, and he was running out of options. There were plenty of trees still halfway standing, but without a saw, he had no way of getting more wood.

Wiping the sweat from his brow, he sat down and took a deep breath. He had checked on Ty about ten minutes ago and the boy was resting comfortably. He needed to clean his wound, but he didn't want to expose it and get it infected. It needed to breathe, and Ryan shivered at the thought of the bone protruding from Ty's arm.

Looking toward the mountain range to the west, his heart skipped a beat. Standing, he took a few steps forward, his eyes widening. The *same* cloud formation was brewing as days before when the monster tornado barreled through and turned the area into an apocalyptic wasteland. He swung open the cellar door and carried the ropes and pieces of wood down, unwilling to risk them being blown away in whatever nature was about to throw them.

Ty lifted his head off the lawn chair, groggy as he rubbed his eyes. "Daddy, what's wrong?"

"Nothing, Son. Just putting some stuff down here so I can work on it in case it rains again."

"Is another storm coming?" Ty's voice shook.

"I don't know, Ty. Don't worry. You're safe down here. I mean

CHAPTER EIGHT

it when I say I won't let anything happen to you." He felt guilty enough about the present situation.

Climbing to the top of the cellar, he tied one end of the rope to the inside of the door, securing it as best as he could. Streaming it down to the floor, he searched for something strong enough to tie the other end to and serve as an anchor that could stand up to the high winds. The only thing available was a pipe in the corner where he had meant to put a sink in. It was another unfinished project to add to his growing list, but now, it served as a beneficial ingredient in his plan to keep the cellar shut off from what was about to transpire above them.

Ryan hoped the knots would stay strong. He didn't tie it up yet. He wanted to get one more look at the weather. Peeking through, he pulled himself up, keeping one eye on Ty and one on the sky. Clouds swirled and he could swear they were growling as they brewed up another disastrous system that would finish the job and kill those who were lucky enough to make it through the first storm.

It was like a bad wreck he couldn't stop looking at. He wanted to see as much of it as he could and get down in the cellar in the nick of time, but he had Ty to think about and the promise he had made to his child. Rain splattered the soaked ground, and he expected it to be cold, but it was warm, splashing on his skin and through his thin tank top.

"Daddy!" Ty yelled at him, and Ryan ignored him, watching the clouds that looked alive, hungry to suck up whatever was in their path. "Daddy!"

Ty yelled again, pulling Ryan from his trance. Slipping back inside, he anchored the door, tying it to the pipe. Was it buried deep enough to stand strong? They would soon find out.

Ryan picked up the lawn chair with Ty still in it, pushing it back against the wall farthest from the door, and sat beside him, holding his hand, probably squeezing too tight. He wasn't a praying man, but he closed his eyes and thought about the words of the *Lord's Prayer*. Hopefully, Cecilia, her parents, and his father were all in a storm shelter somewhere, perfectly safe.

The metal door bounced up and down from the small amount of slack the homemade rope had in it. When he lifted the door up, a few drops of rain came in, but the metal fell, sealing them inside. Ryan watched the rope being pulled tight and loose multiple times, making it weaker each time it happened. He thought about pulling it tight, but the strength of the storm would be no match for him, and he didn't want to risk being sucked out with it.

The metal bounced up and down but provided a good barricade. Ryan stayed up against Ty, partly to comfort the boy and partly to shield him. He never figured out what had injured him before, and he didn't want to take any chances this time around. The clank of the metal was loud, echoing against the roar overhead. A few pieces of rope snapped, but the middle strand was standing strong. If the storm lasted much longer, it'd break and the piece of metal would fly off, leaving them vulnerable again.

"I'm scared!" Ty cried, the tears flowing down his cheeks as he buried his face in Ryan's arm.

What Ryan wanted to say was, "Me too", but he refused to show weakness. The storm stopped as soon as it started, but he knew better than to check it out. It always came back for round two, so he stayed where he was, observing the rope, making sure it was okay. It dripped with water from the rain that was able to get in, but they were much better protected than the first time when nothing was blocking the exit.

Everything seemed calm. There was no rain, no rumbles of thunder, and the wind was gone. Ryan waited another ten minutes, double-checking Ty who was so scared that he was shaking.

"You okay, Son?" Ryan ran his hand down Ty's face.

"When is it going to stop? I want to go home, Daddy. I want Mommy."

"Me too. And I can't answer that. I'm sorry."

"My arm hurts. My head hurts. I don't feel very well."

Ryan kissed his forehead. "I know, Ty. I'm trying to get you some help."

He gently took Ty's arm out of the sling and pulled the bandage away. He used hand sanitizer on his hands, cleaning them enough to handle Ty's wounds. Dabbing some rubbing alcohol on a cotton ball, he wiped it near where the bone was and Ty let out a yelp, but he didn't have much energy, and couldn't pull away. Doing the same to Ty's head wound, he tossed the used gauze into a trash bag.

"We are going to leave the bandages off for a little while and let you get some air."

"But I'm breathing air. What do you mean?" Ty's words came out in pants and his eyelids seemed heavy.

"Your wounds, Ty. I just want to make sure they don't get infected." Ty was so innocent, and even then, he was clueless about the condition he was in. That was probably for the best. He didn't need to know how much trouble they were in.

The edges of the cuts were red, and he had done his best to clean them without causing more pain for Ty, but it felt like a half-ass attempt. The bone worried him the most – what if Ty lost his arm because of this? And the head wound was worrisome too. At least he was alert and talking, but didn't people seem fine days after and then suddenly take a turn for the worse? The thought made Ryan feel like he had swallowed a brick.

"Am I going to die?" Ty asked, looking up at his father.

"No. What did I tell you earlier?" Ryan fanned his fingers through Ty's hair. "I'm not going to let anything happen to you. I'm sorry that you're hurt." Ryan felt the warmth gather in the corners of his eyes and turned his face away. He couldn't let Ty see the tears.

He had to go find help, but he couldn't leave Ty. With the looters and the unpredictable weather, it was out of the question. He could get him out of the cellar and cart him to town where more people were probably gathered. But they lived too far away to make that trek without the absolute certainty that they'd be protected when another storm came through. The question wasn't *if,* it was *when*. There would be more weather. It was like they were stuck in a cycle that was out to kill everyone, controlled by something that was using atmospheric warfare to take over. If he carried Ty off and away from shelter and food and another storm came, they'd be dead.

He needed a vehicle. He needed the atmosphere to calm down. He needed to find Cecilia. And most of all, he needed medical attention for Ty. Help wasn't coming. *No one* was coming. They were forgotten – stuck in hell on earth with no signs of anything getting better.

CHAPTER NINE

Darryl saw the storm forming to the east. He was about two miles from his house and would never make it back in time if the weather decided to backtrack and come his direction. It got dark and the clouds grew faster than he had ever seen.

Looking around, he had no shelter anywhere nearby to go to. There were groves of trees that had already been torn apart, their trunks the only thing still rooted in the ground like a lumberjack had hacked away at the limbs.

Leaning on one, he took a second to watch the sky. He couldn't continue his trek to the south without getting closer to the instability. If he stood back, he'd have a chance to survive if the storm took a normal pattern, leaving him on the west end out of harm's way. But none of the storms had been doing that. From what he had observed, everything swung around at a south-westward direction, and the path was unpredictable.

Sipping his canteen, he sloshed the water around. This was why he struggled with his decision to leave his property. He also worried about Ryan – the storm was right over the Harper Springs area, and they were probably getting hit head-on. From his vantage point, he couldn't see any wall clouds or funnels dipping down, but there was some defined rotation that could easily produce something tornadic at any second.

He could walk west and put even more distance between him and the storm, but that would set him back. It'd also be possible that he'd run into the looters again, and this time, he might not be as lucky as he was the first time he encountered them. If he stayed where he was, his risk of being right in the path grew, especially if it took a more northerly track.

Despite the grim situation playing out in front of him, Darryl admired the show that mother nature was putting on. It was hypnotic watching the different colors mesh together, the lightning flashing from cloud-to-cloud, and the chemistry of the atmosphere blending to form something with that kind of power. A large white hail shaft was right in the middle, and he'd be willing to bet it was producing at least softball-sized hail.

It gave him a natural high, but the loud clap of thunder pulled him from his daze, and he thought about all the innocent people in harm's way. The storm was no longer beautiful when considering how many people would perish.

The wind picked up and cool air sucked up into the clouds. It sprinkled some, but only enough to make the ground wet again, and then it stopped. The storm continued to move northeastward, giving no indication that it would backtrack. With the uncertainty of it all, Darryl questioned his ability to track it, but it pushed off, leaving a lighter gray sky behind it. It was small compared to the recent storms, which was shocking. This would've easily been ranked a severe storm on a normal afternoon. But things were not normal, and he feared they never would be again.

He had to keep going. With as fast as it was moving, he'd never catch up to it unless it stalled out. Getting to Ryan and his family was important, but he also feared what he might find. What if they were dead? What if he stumbled on their bodies? With how desolate and quiet everything was around him, the chances of even finding them at all were minimal. Not knowing

CHAPTER NINE

what would happen next was killing him, and it was disheartening knowing that the only other people he had come across were looters who had already killed his neighbors. Darryl didn't want to admit that things were that bad. It was the twenty-first century. How could it *ever* get that bad?

RYAN SPENT most of the day stringing together rope to make a stretcher. With the stronger pieces of wood, he'd be able to make something sturdy enough for Ty when the time came to get him out of the cellar. It seemed more efficient than wasting his time on steps that would possibly collapse with the next round of storms that came through. All he needed to do was make sure there was a way to safely secure Ty when he pulled him up and not risk the boy falling.

With his fear of leaving the boy unattended, he hadn't strayed far from their shelter. He wondered what was out in the pasture from all the debris that had been tossed around. Maybe he'd find some random parts and things he could use as tools, but with Ty in and out of consciousness, the unpredictable weather, and the looters, he wasn't comfortable going very far.

Leaning over the entrance to the cellar, he flashed his light down inside. "Hey, Ty! You awake?" He needed rest, but he also needed to monitor how often Ty slept. He flashed the light to the side of the lawn chair so he wouldn't blind him.

Ty nodded and murmured something and that was enough response to make Ryan focus on the homemade stretcher. He hoped he'd never have to use it. Maybe the Red Cross would come with their official equipment and whisk him to a good hospital away from the hell they were living.

If it wasn't for his watch, he'd have no idea what time of day it was. It was cloudy and dark most of the time, and he hadn't seen the stars for days. The only time he saw the sun was when the cap had burned off and allowed the dry line to retreat, triggering the storms that left them in the apocalyptic aftermath.

Yawning, he decided to call it a night. It was a little after eight and he was hungry and tired, and he had to come up with a plan on what they needed to do next.

Sliding the branches and wood inside the cellar, he secured the metal door, tying it back to the metal pipe that had held securely during the last bout of weather. Applying a can of propane to a lantern, it brightened their cave enough for him to pull out a few options for their dinner.

He took out a can of tamales and opened them, thankful most canned goods had the tab on them now. He had a pocketknife if he needed it, but it was much more convenient to pull the lid off. Scooping the food into a camp saucepan, he lit the stove and watched them heat up, his mind racing in several different directions.

Ty lifted his head off the lawn chair, his eyes halfway open. "What are you making?"

"Tamales. Want some?"

"I'm thirsty."

Ryan handed him a bottle of water. "Are you hurting?"

Ty nodded and took a few sips. "My arm and my head hurt."

"In about an hour, you can take a Tylenol. Think you can make it until then?" Ryan glanced down at his watch. An hour was an eternity when someone was in pain, but he couldn't risk hurting Ty even more by giving him too much medicine.

Ty set the water on the floor and closed his eyes. "I don't feel good..." he whimpered, and a few tears escaped his eyelids, trailing down his cheeks, leaving lines in the dirt that was caked on his skin. They hadn't cleaned up in several days and it was showing.

Ryan kissed him on the forehead. "I know. I'm working on it, I promise."

Scooping the tamales onto a paper plate, he sat on the floor close to Ty and offered him a bite, which surprisingly, he took, scarfing down the processed junk food. Ryan laughed. Just days before he was cringing at the thought of eating something so atrocious, and here they were, gobbling it up like it was gourmet food.

The tamales made him think of Cecilia. He had to tell himself she was somewhere safe with ample food supply, or he'd panic and make a bad decision to go off and look for her. Offering the last bite to Ty, he tossed the paper plate in a trash bag and gulped some water.

"You ready to get some sleep?" Ryan adjusted Ty's blankets and ruffled his hair. "I bet you're loving not having to brush your teeth."

"Or take a bath," Ty replied, smiling.

"Yeah, we're starting to stink up the place, aren't we?" Ryan laughed and ran his tongue over his teeth, longing for some toothpaste. "I guess we can pretend we are out camping at Fox Lake like we did last summer. You caught so many fish. You beat your old man!"

Ty smiled again and lifted his head. "Will we get to go back to the lake soon?"

"I'll make sure we do, Ty. As soon as we get you well again, we'll go as much as you want." Ryan looked away, wiping another tear from his cheek. If they ran out of food, he'd have to go to the river to try and catch some fish. At least it was an option if it came down to that. "I'm going to shut this lantern off so we can sleep. If you need anything at all, Son, I'm right here beside you."

"Okay, Daddy. I love you."

"I love you too."

He checked the rope that secured the door to make sure the knot was tight and slid onto his lawn chair, clasping his hands behind his head. He stared up into the darkness, smelling the damp walls around them, attempting to process everything. There was no way to get his mind to shut down for a second. Tomorrow would be another day of hoping someone would find them.

Exhaustion won the battle, and he felt his body doze off, drifting into a dream-like state that took him away from the wasteland that was now home.

RYAN WOKE up to Ty screaming. Falling off the lawn chair, he reached for a flashlight, unable to find it. The child's voice echoed off the walls and when he yelled Cecilia's name, there was a tone of desperation and panic in his words.

"Mommy! Mommy!"

Clicking the light on, Ryan grabbed Ty's hand, holding it as he finally woke up. Confused about where he was, he cringed when he lifted his injured arm.

"Lay still, Ty. Don't hurt yourself. It's me. I'm here."

"Where am I? Where's my room? Where's my house?" His voice got louder with each question.

"I think you're dreaming, Ty. I'm right here." Ryan unscrewed the water bottle from supper and helped him take a drink. "Are you okay, Ty?"

"I want to go home."

His complaints were coming more often, and Ryan couldn't blame him. He had been lying flat on his back for the duration of their time down in the cellar, and he was getting antsy. The kid normally bounced off the walls with endless energy, so this was a whole new world for them.

"I do too. Something good is going to happen today. I know it will."

Ryan checked his watch. It was six AM, which was alarming. He had slept almost ten hours. He must have needed it, and he probably could have slept more, but there was no time to waste.

"You want some oatmeal?"

Ryan fired up the lantern and took inventory of their food. There were a few packets of instant oatmeal left. It was about the only thing Ty asked for, and they'd be out in a few days. There was still plenty of peanut butter and instant coffee, and the Vienna sausages and Spam were in good shape. Canned peaches and pears would also be a good breakfast, and it was something Ty liked.

"I'm not hungry. I don't wanna eat." Ty's voice was whiny, and he continued to cry.

"It'll make you feel better."

"No!"

At least Ty had the energy to fight. Instead of dipping into their food, Ryan made a cup of instant coffee and hoped it'd be enough to hold him over until later. Unfastening the knot, he opened the metal door above them.

"I'm going back up there to get some more work done. Please yell if you need me. I'll be back down soon."

"Why can't I go up there?" Ty pointed with his uninjured arm.

"That's what I'm working on, kiddo. There aren't any stairs for you to walk up, and I can't carry you up with the rope I've been using. I'll drop you and you'll get hurt even worse."

"Is it going to rain again today?"

"I hope not."

Ryan went to ground level and it was still dark out. No stars escaped from the clouds and there was no sign of the moon. The sun normally came up around seven, but the overcast sky would hinder the light from coming through. Gathering his supplies, he ventured a little farther out, hoping he'd find something useful, but came up empty. He debated turning his phone on. Each time he powered it up, it drained the battery, and since it had been off the charger for a while now, it was coming down to only having it on if he was certain it'd work.

Staring down at the blank screen, he wished Cecilia's number would flash on it and she'd be on the other end, confirming she was okay. Gripping it in his palm, he closed his eyes and cursed out loud, hoping the universe would hear his frustrations and finally work in his favor.

"Ryan!"

He heard the familiar voice in the distance and opened his eyes. It was too dark to see who it was, but a man was hurrying down the driveway. His immediately thought it was one of the looters, and he rested his hand on his pocket where the weight of the gun was.

"Ryan!" The man waved, and by his walk, he was even more familiar.

"Dad?" Was it him? Stepping in his direction, he broke out into a run, meeting him halfway between the foundation of the house and the cellar. "Dad, did you walk all the way here from your place?"

"Yeah. I started walking and didn't stop until I got here."

"Are you okay?" Ryan motioned toward the cellar. "I've got some water and food. It's not much, but it'll tide you over until someone comes."

Darryl looked down at the ground and shook his head. "Are you alone? Where's Ty? Where's Cecilia?"

Ryan ducked his head and took a deep breath. The question felt like a wall of bricks toppling over him. "Ty is down in the cellar. He's hurt, Dad. His arm is in bad shape, and he's got a head injury. I've done the best I can... but we need help. We need a hospital." He raked his hands through his sweaty hair. "And Cecilia is missing. I..." Ryan bit his lip to control his emotions. "She went to town the night the first big one came through. I haven't heard from her or seen her since."

"I hate to be the bearer of bad news, Ryan, but no one is coming."

"What? How do you know that?"

"It's like we are the only ones left. It's no man's land out there. I never thought a tornadic system would have that kind of power, but from what I've seen, we are dealing with something massive that no one has ever experienced before. Between my place and yours, I only ran across two other people. And they weren't good people."

"What do you mean?"

"Looters. They killed my neighbors just to get their food supply. We have to be careful. They could be coming this way."

Ryan closed his eyes and hoped that he would wake up from their nightmare, but the harsh reality stared him in the face. "There were a couple of guys that came through here a few days ago, but I was able to chase them off. I didn't think it was that bad, just that emergency services were spread thin, so we'd have to be patient and wait until they got to us. Surely somebody has figured out what is going on and they are sending help."

Darryl stepped toward the cellar. "I wouldn't bet on it. With cell phones down, there's no way to call. And if cell phones are down, other means of communication are out as well. No internet either. We don't even know how much ground these storms covered. With the damage I witnessed on the way over, we can't rule anything out, Ryan. Miles and miles of destruction and death. It could've easily stayed organized enough to go right on into Oklahoma and Kansas, and even other parts of Texas."

"I understand how FEMA and Red Cross can't get in due to the damage, but can't they fly in?" Ryan looked up at the sky. He was afraid of what he might see – the dark clouds threatened them with rain.

"Probably can't get through with the unstable atmosphere. And with all signals down, it's too iffy to fly anyway."

"I wish I could get some news or something. It's like we've been forgotten."

"We've either been forgotten, or we are the last few left to survive. I'd say we were lucky, but I bet that food supply you talked about isn't enough to hold you over much longer, is it?"

Ryan shook his head. "No. A few more days. Maybe a week. I'm eating small portions so Ty can have more to keep his strength up, but he has lost his appetite. I was hoping someone would be here by now. It never crossed my mind that no one would come or that this weather system had the capability of killing off everyone from here to Canada. I still don't think it did." Ryan piled up a few more branches, his plans of using them seeming ridiculous now. Looking back at his dad, he clenched his jaw. "Do you really think that we are cut off from the rest of the world?"

Darryl stared off toward the mountains and took a second to answer. "Yes, that's what I'm thinking. But honestly, I think we're dealing with something unprecedented. If it was normal, the National Weather Service would have been on top of it, and we wouldn't be in this situation. Best case scenario is that they're working on getting to us, but since I'm being honest, I'll say this much – it's gonna get a hell of a lot worse before it gets better."

CHAPTER TEN

Ryan sat in a lawn chair across from his dad and Ty. He was good with his grandson, and it seemed to lift the child's spirits when he saw his grandfather shimmy down the side of the cellar. Ryan couldn't get his mind to slow down. His father had never acted crazy before. It took a lot to get him riled up. Hearing him talk like he had about the storms was probably credible, but Ryan had to keep hope that someone out there was working to get to them.

He finished off some potted meat and tossed the metal can in a trash bag. He was stockpiling what he could, viewing the world from a hoarder's perspective, thinking he could use everything in some way. The lid could be used as a knife if he could maneuver it enough to make a blade.

Now that his father was there, they'd go through their supplies quicker. He hadn't eaten much and made sure Ty had what he needed, but Ryan couldn't deny the man food. Sifting through the bags, he wished he had bought more that day at the grocery store, but who would have made plans to be stranded for an undetermined amount of time? Preparing for a few nights was one thing, but issues after tornadoes were resolved quicker than this in normal circumstances.

Kneeling beside Ty, he handed him some water. "How are you feeling?"

"I'm hurting. Grandpa looked at my arm."

"Yeah? And what did he say?" Ryan glanced up at Darryl and back to his son.

"I just said that we need to clean it up again." Darryl stood up and motioned Ryan away from Ty, his brow creased in worry. "It's infected, Ryan. And his eyes... his pupils aren't dilating."

"How am I supposed to keep him from sleeping? What do you think we need to do?"

"He's resting and that is good. His arm concerns me. How in the hell did it happen?"

Ryan didn't like Darryl's accusatory tone, but it wasn't the time or place to argue with him. "I'm not sure. We got down in the cellar and after the storm passed over, I saw him like that. I've felt so guilty about it. I thought I got him down here in time, and we were safe." Ryan scrubbed his palm down the side of his face, feeling his thick whiskers growing into a beard. "I've debated what I should do. Do we leave the cellar and risk being out there when another storm comes? Do we abandon our food and water? And I sure as hell wasn't going to leave him alone!" Ryan's voice echoed off the damp walls.

"I know, Ryan. It's a tough spot to be in, and I wish I could tell you what to do."

"And Cecilia... son of a bitch! How in the hell can something like this happen?" Ryan had been on the verge of losing his cool for a few days, and suddenly, in front of his dad, he let out his frustration. "How can someone not be coming for us?"

"Maybe they are. Maybe I'm wrong about the whole thing and it's just taking some time. I'm sorry about Cecilia."

"You talk like you know for certain she's dead."

Darryl shook his head. "I don't know that, Ryan. I didn't say that."

Ryan took a deep breath and leaned against the wall. "I know. I'm sorry. I wish we wouldn't have gotten split up. I wish Ty wasn't hurting. I'm glad you're here. I was worried about you and Cecilia's parents. Maybe she made it to their house." It was a fat chance. Fox Lake was out of the way from where she was going.

"We'll figure something out."

Ryan grabbed the rope. "I'm gonna go for a little walk. I've been wanting to go out in my pasture and see if there's anything in the debris that might be useful but haven't wanted to get too far away from Ty. I won't be gone long."

"Be careful. I don't have to tell you about watching for storms."

Ryan patted him on the shoulder and went to the ground level. He wanted to look for supplies, but he also wanted to be alone for a while to gather his thoughts. They couldn't just sit around any longer. With word from his dad on the current situation, the only thing they were doing by waiting was dying slowly. He couldn't sit around and watch Ty be in pain any longer, and he couldn't speculate about where Cecilia might be.

When he went back down into the cellar, Darryl was busy cleaning Ty's arm. The boy was cringing, and his eyes were closed, but he was tough and standing strong through the pain. His father was better at the medical stuff – his years of doctoring animals on the farm probably helped with the experience. Ryan watched for a few seconds, feeling more comfortable about his decision after seeing how well his father was doing with Ty. He was a man Ryan could trust, which was the last ingredient he needed in his plan to try and figure out what they were going to do.

Darryl looked up as he finished with the bandage. "I didn't see you standing there. How long have you been there?"

"Not long. How'd you get him to relax?"

Darryl pulled a silver flask from his pocket. "The wonders of whiskey."

"You didn't..." Ryan cocked his head to the side.

"No, I didn't, but I did use some of it to help clean the wound. Instant numbing effect. Seemed to work on him. Your boy is gonna be a whiskey drinker." Darryl laughed and tossed the dirty bandages aside. Standing, he pushed the flask against Ryan's chest. "Take a drink."

"Nah, I'm good."

"It'll relax you. I'm not saying get trashed on it. It's for medicinal purposes."

Ryan unscrewed the lid and took a swig. It was strong and burned, but he savored the taste. He gave it back to his dad. "I'm going to go get some help tomorrow."

Darryl arched his eyebrow and took a pull from the flask before putting it back in his pocket. "You sure about that?"

"There's no other option. Ty is hurting. He's going to lose that arm and more. You said so yourself. It's infected. And his head..." Ryan felt the burning sensation behind his eyes and fought back the tears. "I gotta find Cecilia. If I stay here, we're gonna die. We can't just keep hoping someone will come. It'll be too late if we go off that alone."

Darryl nodded as they both looked at Ty. "I'm not going to try and talk you out of it. I walked over here and I wanna help."

"And I'm glad you did, otherwise, I would have to stay here and wait it out. I trust you enough to leave Ty with you so I can do this."

"You trust me? It's nice to hear that since we haven't been on the best terms the last few years."

Ryan didn't want to talk about their relationship. That was for another time and place. "When I get back with help, we can discuss all that. But right now, I need to get some rest. I'd like to be positive and say I'll find someone out there fast, but we know the truth."

"It's okay to be a realist. Get some sleep, Son."

After checking on Ty one last time, Ryan turned off the lanterns, secured the rope that held the door in place, said one last good night to his dad, and laid down on his lawn chair. Sleep didn't come. He needed rest, but with all his worries, he thought

CHAPTER TEN

about different scenarios, and how he'd take it if Cecilia was dead.

He'd be devastated, and it wouldn't be good for Ty's health. What if they never got closure? The storm was big enough to send his house flying, leaving no trace of it. There'd be tons of missing people who likely had been carried two counties over to be left for dead in the woods or on farmland.

Laying on his side, he stared off into the darkness. He could hear his father snoring nearby, envying the fact that he had fallen asleep. It was a shame he didn't have a book to read. That was always a good way to get sleepy when insomnia plagued him. He had to come to terms with the fact that tomorrow might be the last time he'd ever see Ty and his father. But at least he'd go down swinging instead of leading them all to the grave without trying.

Balling up his coat, he used it as a pillow, closing his eyes, begging his mind to shut down so he could sleep just a few hours. That was all he was asking for.

"Ryan?"

He squinted, unable to see his father. His body ached from the awkward position he was laying in, and when he sat up, he realized the metal door was off, and a small beam of light was cascading in from above.

"What time is it?" Ryan looked down at his watch, blinking away the blurriness. It was seven fifteen, which meant he needed to get moving.

"Ty had a good night. He seems pretty rested this morning. I went ahead and got up and did a few things and let you sleep. Are you still going to head out today?" Darryl poured some coffee into the percolator and lit the camping stove.

"Yeah. I'm not going to talk myself out of it." Ryan smiled. "I've just been making instant coffee every morning. The percolator makes too much for just me."

"Well, you know me, Ryan. I'll drink twelve cups by myself."

Ryan took a metal mug and sipped the coffee. It tasted twenty times better than the instant stuff, and he polished off two cups, drinking them too fast. It'd be the last time he'd have something that tasty, but he saved the rest for his dad to have.

Ryan gathered up a few bottles of water and some Vienna sausages, potted meat, and crackers. The rest he'd leave for them. The canned fruit was tempting, but it was something Ty enjoyed and needed to keep his strength up.

"Is that enough?"

"Yeah. I plan to follow the river for a while. I can always try and fish if I have to. I got some matches and a lighter so I can make a fire at night."

"Daddy? Are you leaving?" Ty lifted his head, but it fell back on the chair.

Ryan knelt beside him, fluffing his hair. He had to keep cool. If he showed any bit of sadness, Ty would see it. "Yeah, buddy, I'm leaving, but I'll be back."

"Where are you going?"

"I'm going to find Mommy. And I'm going to get help so we can get you out of here and get you feeling better, okay?"

Ty reached his good hand toward Ryan, clasping their fingers together. "I love you. You're coming back, right?"

"Yes, I'm coming back. I'm going to find Mommy and I'm coming back. And things will get back to normal. Grandpa is going to stay here and be with you until then. He's going to take care of you. And you take care of him. Can you do that?"

"I can."

Ryan kissed Ty's forehead. "I love you, Ty. I'll see you soon."

Turning to his father, Ryan shook his hand. Whispering, he said, "I sure hope I don't let y'all down."

"You won't. It takes a man to go do what you're doing. I'll take care of Ty. Be safe, Ryan. Watch the sky. Get to the lowest spot you can find if you're in the path of a storm." Darryl smiled.

"Hell, listen to me. You know what you're doing. You know how to watch the weather."

Ryan pulled him in for a hug. "Love you. Thanks for coming. Thanks for taking care of my kiddo."

"Love you too, Ryan."

The hardest part about leaving was taking the first step. Ryan told himself not to look back. It would make him want to abort the decision and stay there with Ty, but he couldn't do it. Hoisting the backpack, he took a sip of water from the canteen his father gave him. It'd keep the water cooler, and if he did stick by the river, it'd be easy to refill. He still had to ration everything he had. There would come a time when he'd have to go a different direction, and water would be scarce.

The handgun was heavy in his pocket. It was added security against wildlife he might run across, and with looters. He wouldn't hesitate to protect himself if he needed to. Ammunition was limited, but he was a good shot, and hopefully, he wouldn't have to use the gun at all.

It was already hot and humid, so he tied his jacket around his waist. With the extreme fluctuation in temperatures, it wouldn't be wise to get rid of it. His first instinct was to go toward town. There were community storm shelters where people would go if their homes weren't equipped with a safe place. Churches often allowed people in their basements. Maybe people in Harper Springs were able to take cover, even with the lack of warning provided.

Ryan wasn't clear on the timeline of how everything had transpired. Did Cecilia have enough time to make it to town? It felt like she had only left the house a few minutes before the storm barreled down on them.

Now he was starting to second-guess himself. Should he follow the highway instead? Maybe he'd run across a vehicle that he could get running, or maybe someone driving through to help would stop and assist. His father's words echoed in his mind – *No one was coming.* He couldn't believe that. He couldn't accept the idea of the rest of the United States leaving them to die. Something had to give. There would eventually be a break in the atmosphere long enough to fly some planes with supplies and medics in. Someone would eventually send mobile crisis units once they could get past the debris and highway closures.

There was about a mile hike from the river to the highway, and if he went between the two, it'd take longer, but he'd walk across more farms where he might run into someone he knew. Instead of the ten-mile walk to Harper Springs, it'd double, but at that moment, he was going to stick with that plan. There would be fish if he ran out of food, and water so he wouldn't dehydrate himself. There would also be a better chance of running across a cellar or place to hide when more weather came through.

The sun beat down on him like a furnace. It was refreshing to see it for a change, but it was hot and it burned his skin, making sweat pour into his eyes. The sun was a major part of supercells forming. The air fed off daytime heating, and that was his biggest fear. He had a hard time finding where the dryline was. With the drier air, it was probably east of him, and that would keep him safe until it retreated west with squall lines forming along it.

Ryan reached the edge of a small hill that overlooked Brooke's Draw where people would gather to hunt, fish, and camp. It was usually busy with tourists and locals, all taking a break on the weekends, but today, it was like a ghost town. The campground was gone, including the cement picnic tables. A metal sign dangled and swayed in the wind, the sideways letters advertising that it was the best fishing area for forty miles, which Ryan could attest to. He had caught lots of catfish right off the docks.

The silence was eerie. He never thought he'd live to see the day when Brooke's Draw would be vacant, and there it was, with no signs of life, not even a squirrel or rabbit who once infested the small oasis. It was like an atomic bomb had been dropped,

CHAPTER TEN

and an eye-level plume of dust aided in providing a post-apocalyptic feel to the weekend getaway spot.

Wiping the sweat from the back of his neck, Ryan swallowed the lump in his throat. He had only walked for fifteen minutes, and it was enough to confirm what his father had said. Things were worse than he had anticipated. The farther he walked away from his land, the more he realized how serious the situation was. He had to do this for his family. For Ty's injuries. For Cecilia – she *had* to be alive. Ryan wouldn't accept any other possibility.

CHAPTER ELEVEN

Before heading to the highway, Ryan made a detour toward the river. He was only about half of a mile from it, and he needed to cool off. Rather than wasting his water, he'd go for a quick dip to bring his body temperature down and see what he might run across. Like the night before, his mind raced with everything transpiring, but he made sure to keep an eye on the sky. The drastic climb in temperature worried him – if nature could wipe the area off of the map, it would be capable of record-breaking heat.

Staying hydrated and nourished would be his biggest challenge, which was one reason he thought it would be best to stay by the river. He could rig up a fishing pole with a sapling and make fishing wire like how he made the ropes back at his place. He wasn't at that point yet. He had enough food for a while, and it was the lack of water that was concerning.

What he'd give for his cell phone to work for at least thirty seconds. Pulling it from his pocket, he checked it, and there was still no signal. He went ahead and tried to call out, but it wouldn't respond. Ending the call, he tried 911. The major cell phone companies always claimed that you could make an emergency call even if the phone had no service, including if the phone wasn't even hooked up to a network carrier.

No luck. Shit! He wished one thing would go his way. He felt like he was in quicksand. One step forward and two steps back.

When he reached the river, he was expecting to see other people there. It was just as vacant as Brooke's Draw. People were normally lined up along the banks, fishing, and tubing on the water. Ryan questioned if the water would be safe to drink. He thought about all the end-of-the-world movies he had watched, and for some reason, the water always seemed to be tainted and killed you as fast as poison.

Dipping his hand in it, it was cooler than he expected, considering the blazing sun beating down on him. It appeared to be clear with no infestation, but what did he know? Amoebas and germs couldn't be seen with the naked eye, so he went off basic instinct, and it was to get in and cool off.

Pulling his shirt off, he stripped to his boxers, stacking everything on the bank beside his bag. He worried someone might come up and take his stuff, but with no human presence for miles, he relaxed. He was aware of the looters, and he'd stick close by in case they came. He didn't want to put too much distance between him and his gun.

The water was refreshing, and he dove under, enjoying the coolness on his skin. When he came back up, he checked in all directions – still no sign of anyone but him. Not even any animals were coming to take a drink, which also made him wonder about the quality of the water. He waded through the river, getting back to shore.

The sky to the west was darkening again and the wind picked up. That was the dryline retreating, just like Ryan had predicted earlier. He put his shirt and pants back on, allowing the fabric to soak up the excess water on his skin. It'd help cool him with the breeze, but his biggest concern was the storm forming quickly.

He needed to find a place to go. He didn't see any shelters on the way to the river, but he knew of a small farm not far from where he was. He didn't know the family well, but it didn't matter – in a time like this, they'd surely let him down underground with them.

Rain began to fall, but it was light. Lightning rumbled in the distance and Ryan couldn't chance it. Breaking into a sprint, he weaved between trees, his heart thumping with the rhythm of his feet on the ground. He could hear the hail slamming against the ground, and it wasn't far behind him. The hailstones came down like bombs flying out of a huge spaceship, and if he slowed his pace down, he'd be pummeled with shards of ice that were so big, they couldn't be classified.

To his left, a tree was struck by lightning and engulfed in flames. The thunder was so loud that it knocked Ryan back, and how he hadn't gotten hit by hail or lightning was nothing short of a miracle. His destination wasn't far away, and his lungs burned, his legs ached, and it felt like it was getting farther away instead of closer.

It was hard to see through the rain, but it looked like a man was standing near the cellar, holding the door open, motioning toward Ryan. Was it an invitation to go? He wasn't going to question it, even if the man denied him, he had to fight his way in.

The mud was thick under his boots, slowing him down. The bag of supplies he had gathered back home was making it heavier, but he couldn't shed the weight. Everything he carried was beneficial, and if he lost it now, his whole plan would fail, and he'd let both Ty and Cecilia down. That was his inspiration to keep running and get to safety.

"Come on in!" The man yelled, pointing down the stairs.

Ryan finally reached him and took the steps two at a time. The door overhead slammed behind him, and though he didn't know the family well, the man who had invited him in looked oddly familiar. He couldn't place him, and when Ryan turned to see everyone else, something told him he was probably better off out in the storm than where he was at that moment.

He recognized the men from somewhere. They weren't from Harper Springs, but maybe they were residents of Fox Lake he had seen in passing when he'd visited Cecilia's parents. That didn't seem right either.

"Well, if it isn't the man who pulled his gun on us!" One of the men nudged the other. "What brings you here?"

It hit Ryan blindside. They were the guys who tried to steal his supplies. Taking a few steps back, he noticed another man in the corner, but he definitely didn't belong with them. He looked terrified, as if he couldn't get far enough away.

"I'm not here to cause trouble," Ryan said. Holding his hands at eye level, he tried not to draw attention to his backpack. They'd rob him blind if they knew what was inside.

"Again, I ask, what are you doing here? Run out of food?"

The metal door above them banged against the frame and rain pattered so hard that Ryan could barely hear him. Looking up, he wondered how they managed to get it to stay put.

"I am looking for help." He was cautious to give too much information away, but maybe it'd make them more sympathetic if they knew his whole story. "My son is hurt, and we haven't heard from anyone in days. I'm also trying to find my wife."

"Help isn't coming," the other man chimed in. "We told you that when you pointed that gun in our faces! You won't be doing that to us again!"

Ryan shook his head and looked at the other man whose eyes were as wide as saucers. "No, like I said, I'm not here to cause trouble, and I thank y'all for letting me come down here and get out of the storm. It looked like another bad one and..."

"Would you shut up! We're not here to help anyone!"

"Is it really that bad that you're turning on everyone so fast?" Ryan wasn't sure if it was the best question to ask, but it fell out of his mouth before he could even think about it. "Can't we all work together and get some help?"

"He doesn't get it, does he?" One man spoke to the other and they both laughed. "No one is coming. We are all on our own.

And if it means me killing you to live, I'm not going to think twice. Now, what do you have in that bag?"

Ryan slid it off his shoulder and unzipped it. How could he have let this happen? He was desperate to find a shelter and not get killed by the storm. Instead, he had been shoved into the looter's world where he might not come out alive from it, either.

"Empty it slow. If I see any signs of a gun, I'm going to beat the shit out of you, do you understand?"

Ryan did as he was told, thankful he kept the gun in his pocket and his jeans were baggy. If they tried to take it, he'd draw the line there. He squatted and emptied the beef jerky, potted meat, and crackers, as well as a jar of peanut butter and several bottles of water. The last can of tamales rolled beside the pile food, and his heart ached for Cecilia. Finding her now felt impossible.

"Looks like we hit the jackpot!"

"You're not taking my stuff," Ryan said, gritting his teeth. He was trying to stall. The storm above was still raging. What he imagined was hail was slamming on the door, and the wind sounded like a freight train. What hadn't been destroyed yet would be completely gone once he got back to ground level.

"Oh, we're not, huh? How do you figure?"

When Ryan looked up, he was staring down the barrel of a shotgun. He slowly straightened his posture and held his hands up again. They didn't have a gun the first time he met up with them, but there was no telling how many people they had taken things from.

"Not such a big talker now, are you?"

"Take the food. There's no reason to keep us, though." Ryan motioned toward the other man who stayed against the wall, his chest rising and falling fast.

"No? I should blow you away for being such a damn headache. And then we'll go back to your cellar where your little boy is and finish the job. Just think of it as us putting you out of your misery. Everyone who didn't die in the tornadoes will eventually die of thirst and hunger. Why not let us give you the easy way out?"

"It can't be that bad. Help will be coming," Ryan kept his voice low, the sweat dripping into his eyes, burning them. He blinked to try and clear them, but it didn't help, and he was afraid to move an inch. The looter might have a hair trigger.

"If there is one thing you should believe, it's that they aren't. You ever read Revelations in the bible? It's happening. The world is ending. We've been all over the area. People are dead. Livestock is dead. Life as we knew it before, is over. We started looting early because we want the upper hand. The one who takes charge first is the one who survives."

Ryan scoffed. "I'm not going to get into a philosophical argument with you. You can lower that gun and take my bag. I'm not a threat to you since you're armed."

"You look pretty strong. We could use him for something, couldn't we?" He asked his friend, looking away for a split second. The next time he did that, Ryan had to take a chance and try to gain control. At least he'd go down fighting.

"Yeah, but I think we should just off the son of a bitch. I don't trust him."

Ryan glanced at the other man held hostage and back at the barrel. His heart raced so hard that it was going to thump out of his chest. He knew guns and had used them, but he had never been on the other side of the barrel, knowing in a second, he'd be killed with a simple pull of the trigger.

"Such a damn waste. A strong man like this could be useful, but you're right. We can't be watching his every move. He's smart enough to ruin everything we've done so far. Sorry, not sorry." The looter smiled. "Sorry we couldn't give you a last meal like those ol' boys on death row."

Ryan wasn't sure how he got the courage to do it, but he grabbed the barrel as hard as he could and pulled it, attempting to point it upward, away from everyone. The looter grunted and struggled as they fought over possession of the weapon, both falling to the floor with a hard thud. The man was stronger than Ryan had given him credit for, and again, he was looking down the barrel. He closed his eyes and tried to find the last bit of energy he had, gripping the gun so tight that his knuckles ached. He thought about Cecilia and Ty, and that was his inspiration to fight until death. The other looter tried to break up the fight, but with the shotgun moving around and unstable, he was unable to jump in and help, which worked best for Ryan. Being outnumbered would completely ruin his plan.

After what felt like an eternity, a loud gunshot rang out and Ryan felt the heat through the metal, echoing against the dirt walls of the storm shelter. Everything fell silent, including the rain and hail.

CHAPTER TWELVE

Darryl sat beside Ty's lawn chair and watched him sleep. The health of his grandson was concerning, and his patience was past the breaking point. He hated to think it, but the chances of ever seeing Ryan again were slim. Another storm had come through, and though it wasn't as intense as the ones before, it was enough to do some more damage. Ryan had only left a few hours before and was probably right in the middle of it.

Any chance of having a positive attitude flew out of the window. As it was, Ty and Darryl were the only two left. Ryan's frustrations were spot on – where in the hell was the help that should have been there by now? Plenty of time had passed for someone to get there, which made Darryl fear the worst. The weather was probably an underlying issue among a massive problem that spread farther than west Texas.

Grabbing a bottle of water, he took a sip and screwed the lid back on. He was thirsty, and the moisture soaked into his tongue like a sponge, but he kept his rations small. Ryan had done a good job stocking up the shelter, but he hadn't prepared for the long term, nor did Darryl expect him to. He was shocked his son had done it at all.

He looked over Ty's arm. Below the gauze, it looked like his skin had a blue tint to it. Maybe it was his imagination or the lighting – the lanterns lit the cellar up just enough to see, so maybe it wasn't as bad as it appeared.

He studied everything Ryan had worked on before he got there. He had braided together switches from branches and made rope, and he had gathered wood. The game plan was to get Ty out and to a hospital, and the wood was likely piled up to rebuild the steps so they could get him out once they were able to leave.

"Grandpa?" Ty lifted his head from the lawn chair, his eyes half open.

"Yeah, buddy, I'm right here."

"When is Daddy coming back?"

"I hope he comes back soon."

Ty lay his head back. "And he'll get me out of here when he does?"

"Yes, Ty, maybe even before that." Darryl felt the warmth gather in the corner of his eyes. He didn't have the heart to tell the boy that the chances that his father would ever make it back were slim. It killed him to think that Ty would end up an orphan because Cecilia had probably been killed in the first storm. Based on what Ryan had told him, she never stood a chance.

"Why do you look so sad, Grandpa? If Daddy is getting help, we should be happy."

If only everyone saw the world through a child's eyes, none of this would have been so frustrating. "I'm not sad, Ty. Just a little tired. How are you feeling?"

"My head hurts."

"And your arm?"

"I can't feel it."

"You can't feel it?" Darryl sat up. Maybe it *was* blue like he had thought. Was the circulation cut off?

"No, it doesn't hurt anymore, and when I try to move it, I can't feel anything."

CHAPTER TWELVE

Darryl knelt beside the chair and gently sat Ty up, being as careful as possible. The child would probably get dizzy from the sudden movement. Slowly moving the arm, he hoped it would get some blood flow. The protruding bone rubbed against the bandage, making Darryl cringe, but it didn't seem to bother Ty.

"Does it hurt now?"

"Nope. Does that mean I'm getting better?"

Ty was going to lose the arm. What could he do to prevent it? "Can you stay sitting up for me, Ty?" He grabbed a blanket and balled it up behind him, helping support his back. "Does it make you feel dizzy to sit that way?"

"Dizzy?"

"You know, like when you get off of the spinning rides at the fair?"

"Yeah, a little." Ty giggled.

The way Ty was acting didn't help Darryl's concerns. With a head injury, Ty could take a turn out of nowhere. His sudden change in mood meant that something was going on in his skull, or he was just being goofy because his arm wasn't bothering him, and he confused it with feeling better.

"Drink some water." Darryl offered him the same bottle he had just opened. "I want you to drink as much as you can. And tell me if you start to feel your arm."

"I don't *want* to feel my arm. It didn't feel good."

"I know. Can you move your fingers for me?"

Ty complied with Darryl's request, but they only wiggled for a moment. "It feels like when my feet fall asleep."

That was a good thing. It meant the blood was starting to move. "Good! Keep moving them, okay?"

Darryl made sure they had enough ibuprofen and Tylenol. If Ty gained feeling in his arm again, he wanted to keep a handle on it. He wouldn't wish that kind of pain on anyone, and he wouldn't be able to live with himself if the boy did lose the use of the arm.

Spilling out one of the pills in his palm, he broke it in half and handed it to Ty. "Take this."

"Daddy gave those to me when I was hurting. I'm not hurting." He shook his head and drank some of the water, spilling some down his chin.

"I know, Ty, but you aren't hurting because you took them. If we stop now, your arm might bug you again." Why were kids so hardheaded about taking pills?

Ty opened his mouth and Darryl put it on his tongue. He swallowed it with a gulp of the water and Darryl wondered if the painkillers were doing internal damage. It was adult medicine, and hopefully breaking it in half would reduce the chances of liver damage and stomach problems.

"Are you hungry, Ty?"

"No."

"You should probably eat something soon. Gotta stay strong, okay?"

Darryl looked at their options. It was food he'd never touch under normal circumstances, but today, it all looked delicious.

RYAN HAD TO ACT FAST. The looter who held the gun on him was lying in a pool of blood, his eyes glossy and staring off into oblivion. The other looter was still alive and lunged at him, but Ryan was able to grab the shotgun, aiming it at the other man. His index finger was on the trigger, ready to pull it, but the nuisance backed off, looking down at the lifeless body at his feet.

Ryan was still on the floor, and he stood up, keeping the gun trained on him. Everything had happened so fast that he couldn't remember how the gun got turned back on the looter. His eyes were closed during the fight, and finally, a stroke of good luck worked in his favor. He had come out on the winning side, and with the handgun in his pocket and the shotgun in his possession, there was no way he'd lose now.

CHAPTER TWELVE

"You shot my brother, you son of a bitch!"

Ryan felt guilty, but it was replaced by a desire to live. He had his own family to think about, and had he not taken control of the situation, it would have been him on the floor in his own blood.

"Your brother got himself killed." He checked the other man in the corner, and he hadn't moved. He was pressed up against the dirt wall, unable to get far enough away. At least he hadn't gotten hurt in the altercation.

"Then you better kill me, because when I get the chance, you're a dead man."

"Not the smartest thing to say with a gun pointed at you," Ryan replied, unsure of what to do with him. He couldn't kill him now. The man wasn't an immediate threat, and he wouldn't have the heart to pull the trigger unless it was self-defense. But he also didn't want him running loose with the constant worry of him coming after them.

"So, what are you gonna do? Call the cops?"

"I'm taking this man and we're leaving. And don't follow us." It was probably stupid, but Ryan wasn't a killer. The fact that the other looter was dead tore at him, even if he was protecting himself. "Come with me." Ryan motioned toward the stranger, his trust on high alert. He hated being in full-on survival mode and couldn't believe what the thieves had said about help not coming, but it seemed plausible with how everything was escalating so quickly.

The man pushed off the wall and extended his hand. "My name is Steve. Steve Tarrant."

"Ryan Gibson. You from around here?" He seemed familiar, but the name didn't ring a bell.

"Just moved here from Oklahoma. Bought the old ranch down the road from here. Wasn't in the house two months when the weather went crazy on us. We have some pretty crazy stuff happen where I'm from, but nothing ever like this."

Ryan looked through the cabinets and filled his bag with food.

It wasn't much, but he couldn't pass it up. "Believe me, Steve, I don't think anyone has ever seen anything like this. Don't let it ruin Texas for you." He winked and tried to insert some humor, but it fell flat. They were in deep shit and both men knew that.

Pulling out a drawer, Ryan found another handgun and a box of ammunition that went with it. He also found a few more shotgun shells. He wouldn't leave any of that behind. Guns were common and most people in the area owned them, but now they were like precious gold, and taking them out of the looter's hands would make everyone a bit safer. There were two cans of spray paint, and though he didn't know what he'd need them for, he put them in his bag. Simple everyday items were now rare finds, and he suddenly understood the mindset of a hoarder.

Turning to the looter, Ryan pointed the shotgun at him again. "I'm leaving some food for you."

"Why in the hell would you do that?"

"Because I'm not an animal like you and your brother. If I find out you are out causing problems again, I won't hesitate to blow you away, you hear me?"

The looter backed against the wall and nodded. "You say you're looking for your wife?"

"Yeah."

"What's she look like?"

Ryan scoffed and hesitated to answer him. "Why do you wanna know?"

"I might've seen her when I was out there."

"Where?"

"With another group of people. There were like five of them."

"How about *you* describe who you saw, and I'll let you know if it was possibly my wife?" Ryan asked.

He described a woman that resembled Cecilia. "It's your wife, isn't it? I did see her. She wasn't in good shape. Looked like another group of looters, so me and my brother steered clear."

"Where were they headed?"

"North, last time we saw them, but that was days ago."

Ryan gripped the gun and clenched his jaw. "Why would they be keeping her?"

"That's for you to figure out. I was going to use you and this other guy here to help rebuild, sort of like slaves to make a new place to live. Maybe they have the same idea. Or maybe she decided to stay with them. Maybe she figures it's her only way to survive. Being out there alone is a death sentence."

Ryan ducked his head and took a deep breath. If the woman he spoke of was Cecilia, she had been spotted alive. Now he had to make up time and get to her. Or the looter could be leading him on a wild goose chase to throw him off course as a way of revenge for his brother's death.

"You better not be lying."

"I guess you'll never know." His evil smile was back, making the hair on the back of Ryan's neck stand up. "Just like you'll never know if I'll track your ass once you leave."

That should have been enough to give Ryan the courage to shoot him, but he still couldn't bring himself to do it. "Don't threaten me."

"Or what?"

Ryan pushed the barrel of the shotgun under his chin, lifting his head. His index finger rested on the trigger, and he looked the man in the eye. "Your brother is dead because he was about to take *my* life, and I have two people depending on me to get help." His voice shook and he tried to mask his emotions. "There's still a chance for you. In times like these, it's better to pull together instead of going around and ruining other people's lives."

"Or be weak and die."

"No. I'm not weak. And I'm not going around kidnapping and killing. I'm going to leave you here. I left you some food. You're on your own. If you want to follow us, go right ahead, but

I've got your guns and all your ammunition. You won't threaten me a third time, do you understand?"

He nodded and backed away, a red spot on his skin the shape of the end of the barrel. No one said a word. The only sound was the wind whipping overhead. Ryan started up the steps, adjusting his backpack which was a bit heavier from the supplies he collected.

"You coming, Steve?" He still had to feel him out, but he didn't seem like he was a bad guy.

When they got to ground level, Steve pointed at a padlock beside the door. "They locked me in there when they'd go out to loot."

Ryan slammed the door and dust flew up around them. Latching the lock to the metal, he secured the man inside. Pulling a can of spray paint from his bag, he painted a large red circle on the cellar, alerting help that someone was inside. He couldn't live with himself if no one ever came, but he also couldn't take any chances.

"In the fire department, we are trained to look for signs like this in times of disaster. X means someone is dead inside. Anything else means help is needed. Someone will come for him. Right now, he needs to stay put. The fewer jackasses like him running around, the easier it'll be for us to do what we need to do." Ryan mainly said it to justify his decision. There was a man dead inside, but with one still living, search and rescue would respond faster with the circle. It was too late to go back on it now. He didn't have the key and had no clue where it was. The looter was locked inside with several days of food and water.

"What exactly do we need to do?" Steve asked.

"You got any family?"

"It's just me. Recently divorced. My ex-wife stayed in Oklahoma."

Ryan hiked up the driveway, and Steve followed. Too much time had passed, and he had to get away from what just happened. With daylight burning and the possibility of more storms, they had to keep moving.

"Any kids?"

Steve shook his head. "None."

"I've got a boy. He's hurt. It's serious."

"Where is he?"

"Back at my place with my dad. We got in the cellar just in time, but..." Ryan wiped the sweat gathered on his neck with his hand. "I gotta find help. He might lose his arm."

"I'm sorry to hear that. And your wife?"

"I'm not sure if I can take the guy seriously. He could've just been saying that to give me false hope." Ryan watched the clouds over the mountain range. They didn't look too ominous yet.

"I was with them when we saw the group. He described the woman correctly. I don't think she was with looters. It was hard to tell."

"Lots of women could look like that, but I'm going to hold onto it and say that it is Cecilia. I don't have much else to go on, so one glimmer of hope will be enough motivation for me to head north and find her."

Steve patted him on the back. "I'd like to help. I have nothing else going on. I'd rather not just sit around and wait. Doesn't look like anyone is coming for us anyway."

Ryan hoped that was one thing the looters were wrong about. How could *no one* be coming?

CHAPTER THIRTEEN

The sun was setting over the mountain range and the heat of the day was finally fading. It made for cooler nights, so Ryan found a spot under a grove of trees that hadn't been destroyed. He gathered wood from the fallen limbs and dug a small hole to start a fire. His stomach growled from hunger, and with the extra food he gathered from the looters, he'd eat a little more and enjoy a full stomach for the first time in days.

Pulling the lighter from his bag, he struggled to get the fire going. The wood was wet from the recent rain.

"We might have to do without a fire tonight."

Steve didn't say much. He had been quiet for most of their hike, which Ryan didn't mind. Too much talking wasted energy and as frustrated as he was, would probably grate on his nerves.

Rolling a few pieces of gauze from the small first aid kit he had made, he balled it up under the wood and lit it. It smoked for a bit and finally caught some pine needles on fire. It smoldered and Ryan gently blew on it. A few flames licked the twigs and with patience, a small fire finally started. It wasn't big enough to do much, but if they stayed close, it would provide some warmth. His coat would help, but Steve didn't have anything but the clothes he was wearing. They'd need to try and find him something for protection soon.

"You can sit closer to the fire. If you need to, I can let you use the coat, and we can trade off."

"I'm fine. It's cool out, but nothing I can't handle."

Ryan opened the bag of beef jerky and offered him a piece, and he gladly accepted. The temperature outside was tolerable, but with the extreme fluctuation in the climate and atmosphere, Ryan feared that they'd come across weather where Steve would be vulnerable.

"So, what did you do before the world decided to go crazy on us?" Steve asked, tearing a piece of the jerky off with his teeth.

"I'm a mechanic. Own a shop in Harper Springs."

"Yeah? That's a good skill to have."

"What about you?" Ryan washed the jerky down with a gulp of water. It tasted so good, but he resisted the urge to drink too much.

"I've been a farmer all my life. I heard cotton and milo did well down here, so I figured I'd try my hand at it. And grapes. I didn't realize there were so many vineyards down here."

"It's a new industry that's just getting started in this area. The heat helps the flavor of the grapes. And the soil is perfect. Lots of cotton farmers are transitioning. Seems to be a bigger money maker that doesn't depend as much on the weather." If there were any vineyards still standing, it'd be another way to get some food.

"Talk about irony," Steve said, laughing. "I wonder if my ex-wife has heard about this on the news and is trying to get hold of me. My phone hasn't worked since it all happened."

"With her being in Oklahoma, there's a good chance it all went up her way. What part are you from? I've been up that way a few times myself."

"Near Oklahoma City. Seems to be the bull's eye right in tornado alley."

Ryan nodded and slipped the jerky back into his bag. Grabbing a stick, he prodded the fire, adjusting the logs. It would go out soon and he tried to keep it going, at least, until they were comfortable enough to sleep.

"Something is odd about all of this."

"How so?" Steven asked.

"You see shit like this on the news all the time. All these natural disasters all over the world and none of them seem to take as long in getting help to people. With the way media is now, word spreads fast. What is the exception here? I get that we're in a rural area, but it's been almost two weeks now. This country has a lot of resources – The National Guard, FEMA, The Red Cross... where is everyone?" Saying his concerns out loud made it seem even worse.

Steve leaned back against a tree and looked up at the sky. "All good questions that I wish I had answers to. Maybe this is worse than we know. Maybe it's more widespread than just here."

"Maybe. I'm not a conspiracy theorist by any means, but I think this goes well beyond a crippling weather system." Ryan had to stop himself. If he continued to talk about it, he wouldn't be able to get any sleep, and with all the hiking they were doing, he needed the rest.

"You say you're a mechanic, right?"

"That's right."

"I think I remember seeing a car down by the river right before the looters got me. It was torn up pretty bad and I just saw it in passing, but it might be of some use for us."

A car would cut down travel time and as he had said before, Ryan would take anything positive. "How far from here is it?" He had found a few other cars on his hike, but there would be no chance of him being able to fix them. Maybe this one would be different. He didn't have any tools, but he might not need anything to get it running.

"I'm not sure. I'll be able to tell better in the daylight. Since I'm not from the area, I get turned around easily."

"That's great, Steve. We'll try and find it tomorrow. I'm going to try and get going early before the sun comes up. The more daytime heating the atmosphere has to work with, the better chances of more storms, and if I can get the car running, we can cover a lot more ground."

Ryan laid back against a tree trunk and pulled his collar up around his neck and face. He felt guilty about having a coat, but each time he offered, Steve declined. It was nice having someone walking with him. Though he didn't know the man, talking to another human being pulled him out of reality, even if it was just for a little while. He didn't feel like he was the last man on earth.

Sleep came easier than he thought, and he dozed, his body giving in to the physical exhaustion.

THE FIRST THING Ryan thought about when he woke up was the looter he had locked in the cellar. He wondered when the guilty feelings of taking a life would fade. When he thought about it in terms of survival, it felt a bit more justified, but he still had a hard time grasping that they were already that desperate.

Looking down at his clothing, he was covered in dirt, his beard was growing in thick, and he hadn't washed off since he took a dip in the river. How amazing a nice hot shower would feel, not to mention a big glob of toothpaste on his toothbrush. Slicking his tongue over his teeth was not pleasant, and he reached for his canteen, sloshing water around in his mouth. If they made it back to the river today, he'd wash the layers of dirt and sweat off.

Steve was already up and had a fire going. The scent of coffee wafted toward Ryan, reminding him that he was starving. The percolator bubbled above the flames, spilling some of the coffee over the edge.

"Where'd that come from?" Ryan pointed at the coffee pot. It looked identical to the one he had left with his father.

"Had it in my bag. One of the items I snagged before we left yesterday. A man can't live without coffee." He pulled two metal mugs out of the back pocket and handed one to Ryan. "You drink coffee?"

"Hell yes, I do." Extending it, Steve poured him a mug, and Ryan blew on it, unable to wait for it to cool. Sipping it, it soothed him from the inside – a temporary healing for his aches and pains. It was simple black coffee, but it was like they had just splurged at Starbucks on their most expensive blend.

"I figure it'll give us some early morning energy."

Ryan enjoyed it, trying not to finish it too fast. "I think you're my new best friend, Steve. Thanks for making it."

"What's the point of all of this if we can't enjoy the simple things?"

Ryan lifted the mug in the air as a sign of agreement and poured another cup. They both sat in silence, Ryan lost in thought about the next course of action. He wanted to find the car Steve had mentioned, but he worried it would set them back. What if they came across it and it was so damaged that he couldn't fix it? It would already be a challenge with limited tools and resources. But if he could get it running, it'd be wonderful. He had to try. If it was as damaged as the other cars he had found, he'd just continue with his original plan and keep walking. Eventually, they'd find one that would work enough to get them the rest of the way into Harper Springs.

It would also make them a target if others caught word of a running vehicle, but that was a bridge they weren't even close to crossing yet. Ryan wasn't even sure how many people were still alive. In the past two weeks, he only encountered six people still living, and that included him.

"I think the car I saw was a few miles south of here." Steve pointed behind them. "I know it was by the river. And it was close to the shelter where those guys took me."

"By the river is a good thing. We can replenish our water and cool off when it gets hot." The fact that it was south would mean they'd put more ground between them and where Cecilia had been spotted. He was torn on what to do, but he needed to see the vehicle before he made any other big decisions.

They gathered up their supplies and started walking. The sun was coming up and the temperature was already climbing. Ryan tied his coat around his waist and they both were quiet for a while. He kept a lookout for anything out of the ordinary. There were new concerns for not only the weather, but other people, and wildlife that would be coming around looking for food and water. The area was known mainly for coyotes and foxes, but sometimes mountain lions were spotted.

The shotgun he had acquired made him feel safer because it was stronger than his gun. It conveniently had a strap, which made lugging it around easier.

"You any good at tracking storms?" Steve asked.

"I have to take classes as part of my requirement to be on the fire department."

"Wouldn't you say that looks like something we need to keep our eye on?" Steve pointed toward a massive thunderhead that looked like a nuclear bomb had gone off. It was gray and white, and with the sun on it, it looked like a painting. "It's mighty beautiful, I will say that!"

"Definitely something we need to watch. Right now, it's still miles away and moving away from us, but that doesn't mean we need to take it lightly." Ryan used to love seeing thunderheads, but now it only meant that they'd be running for their lives again. Maybe it wouldn't shift and come their way, but the jet streams seemed to be working against them.

"I remember the grove of trees ahead. The car is about a mile from that if I'm remembering correctly."

Ryan ran the back of his hand over his forehead. It was hot and a nice rain shower would be perfect to cool them off, but there was no such thing as a simple rainshower. It had to come with shards of hail bigger than dogs and winds strong enough to blow away farmhouses. The lack of people around was still concerning. The population of the county was barely over five thousand, but from Ryan's calculations, six out of five thousand was an unreal ratio that he had a hard time accepting.

He pulled his cell phone out of his pocket. It made a nice little jingle as it turned on, and the reception bars were still missing.

"I haven't gotten mine to work either."

"Call me a hopeless optimist," Ryan said, dialing 911. It was the same story – nothing happened, only this time, his phone made a loud beep, warning him that his battery life was down to twenty percent. Searching for a signal drained it quickly, but this time, Ryan didn't seem bugged by it. What good was it if no one was alive to accept his call? He was really starting to believe this was it for them. This was their new way of life, turning into foragers and nomads. Their only way of life was to find food and survive. With so many post-apocalyptic books and movies out, it was a form of entertainment just a few short weeks ago, never dawning on him that it easily could become a reality.

They reached the banks of the river, and the water flowed deeper than Ryan had seen it in years. At least the storms were filling it up. "We getting close?" Ryan asked.

"It's behind those trees! I remember it well." Steve picked up the pace, leading Ryan toward the car.

A few branches had fallen on it and Steve pulled them off, revealing an old Dodge Neon. The windshield was busted out and Ryan's heart skipped a beat when he opened the door, revealing a body in the driver's seat.

"Oh my God..." he whispered.

"What's wrong?" Steve got his first glimpse of what was inside. "Did you know her?"

"That's Mrs. McElroy. She owns the bakery next door to my shop."

CHAPTER FOURTEEN

Ryan pulled more of the fallen branches from around the car, his concern on Mrs. McElroy and not on the extent of the damage to the vehicle. Her eyes were wide and glossy like she had been frightened seconds before she died. There was a piece of wood that had shot through the window, impaling her in the chest. He hoped it killed her quickly, but from the look on her face, she knew exactly what had happened and felt every bit of it.

Blood was soaked in her shirt and dripped onto the seat beside her. She had bled out, and Ryan shook his head, blinking away the warmth in the corner of his eyes.

"Poor woman," Steve said. "How well did you know her?"

"Since I was a kid." Ryan's voice shook and he took a step back. "I wasn't expecting this." He spread his hands, surveying the wreckage. "I guess in the back of my mind I just sort of hoped everyone was hiding and scared to come out. I wonder how many more are dead."

"I'm sorry, Ryan. She looks like she was a nice lady."

Ryan walked to the edge of the river and watched the water flow downstream. It was roaring and deep, and he felt himself on the verge of losing his cool. Finding the car was something good, but he couldn't pull himself together to assess what kind of repairs it would need. Not knowing what was happening was the worst feeling.

He used to scoff at the climatologists who warned the world that everyone was ruining it. Holes in the ozone layer, global warming, and pollution were going to destroy the land before the newest generation had a chance to grow old, and Ryan never took it seriously. Now he felt stupid – nature was damaged and pissed, doing just as the scientists had predicted, taking its anger out on the very things that caused the problems.

It seemed unreal, like a nightmare he couldn't wake up from, but when he glanced over his shoulder, Steve was there, and Mrs. McElroy was dead in the car. Cecilia was missing. How would he handle it if he walked up to her car and found her the same way? Ty was hurt with the possibility of losing his arm, and even worse – what if he had brain damage?

Wiping the tears from his face, he tried to get it together. He couldn't fall apart, or he'd fail too many people who were depending on him. Turning on his heel, he went back to the car, taking a look at it.

"You okay?" Steve asked.

"I'm good. How much do you know about cars, Steve?"

"Enough to know that we have our work cut out for us."

"I'm going to need to pop the trunk. At least the keys are in the ignition."

Ryan moved to the driver's side and looked into Mrs. McElroy's brown eyes, closing her lids as best as he could. Now it looked like she was squinting at him, much like she had done when she offered him free donuts and he declined. What he'd give for one of her pastries right now – gooey chocolate filling and flaky crust. His stomach growled at the thought of it. He couldn't work on the car with her there. She was in the way, and it felt disrespectful.

"Hey Steve, can you help me move her?"

Getting her off the seat was hard. The piece of wood was

impaled through her body and into the seat, and they finally got her free with some force. Ryan lifted under her arms and Steve lifted her legs. They carried her to a tree and laid her in the shade. Ryan looked down at her, still unable to swallow the bitter pill that life was handing him. The wood was still in her chest, and though she was dead, Ryan couldn't bring himself to pull it out. It didn't seem right.

"We'll have a funeral for her. But we gotta move fast. Did you notice the thunderhead you were watching earlier?" Ryan pointed toward the western sky.

"Damn, it's tripled in size."

"And looks to be coming this way," Ryan replied.

Opening the car hood, everything seemed to be in place. Three of the four tires were flat, and the windshield was so busted that he'd just have to knock the whole thing out. Sitting where Mrs. McElroy had died, Ryan tried not to think about it and turned the key. The engine turned over a few times but didn't start. He tried once more but stopped, fearing he'd cause more damage.

"We could drive on the flat tires for a bit, but we'll bend up the rims and that'll completely hinder the car." Ryan ran his hands through his wet hair, feeling the sweat drip on his fingertips and down his neck. "I wonder why it won't start." Ryan looked toward the river and back to the car. "This river rises pretty fast with rain, and with the torrential downpours we've had, it could've gotten up this high."

"Would it retreat that fast?"

"Oh yeah. The river depth fluctuates just as fast as it floods. I'm willing to bet that at least the hood has recently been covered in water. The damn engine is probably flooded."

Steve took a deep breath. "Damn, that's not good."

"I need to disconnect the battery, so it doesn't spark something. And figure out just how deep the river crested. Trying to start it just now probably made moisture go into the transmission and fuel system. I probably compounded the damage."

He looked for a waterline on the car – the water wasn't clear and full of mud, and it looked as deep as the dashboard. Walking to the back of the car, he broke out one of the taillights, and a small splash of water dripped from it. That wasn't a good sign. That meant the river had flooded high enough to damage the electrical system of the car.

"Shit, we've got our work cut out for us. And if that storm comes this way, we might as well forget about it. There's no chance in hell that I can get the engine dried out and repaired before the river rises again. I'll have to change the oil and filters." The car was in bad shape, but at least the frame was still intact, which was better than the other vehicles he had come across.

"I guess we won't be using this car?" Steve asked, leaning over the motor with him.

"I can probably rig something up, but without my normal tools, I'm not sure I can. If I could get my hands on a wrench and some screwdrivers, I could do a temporary fix that would get us a few miles. I'll have to check the bearings and crankshaft seals. They aren't good at keeping stuff out, only in."

"I wish I was better help," Steve said, looking at the sky.

"You are. The first thing we can do is try and move it farther back away from the river. With the flat tires, it's going to be tough, but the farther we get it, the better chance of it not getting flooded again. I would never be able to get it to roll by myself."

Ryan got back in the driver's seat and pushed the brake down. Attempting to put the car in neutral, the shifter wouldn't budge. Pushing down again, he forced it, hoping he didn't cause more damage to his growing list of repairs. With the engine being off, it was almost impossible getting it to go, but finally, after several attempts, the gear indicator moved to N.

Getting out, he stayed by the wheel to help steer it, and Steve pushed against the hood. The ground was muddy, so they didn't make much progress. Ryan pushed as hard as he could, gritting his teeth, partly out of trying to get the car to move, and

CHAPTER FOURTEEN 117

partly out of frustration. Why wasn't anything coming easily? All he wanted was one lousy break that would help them progress forward with *something*!

Keeping one eye on the sky, he wasn't willing to give up just yet. With time passing, he might as well try and work on the car. It wasn't going anywhere, and he had to keep hope for something, otherwise, he'd go crazy.

"Push, Steve! If we could get it out of these muddy ruts, we might gain some traction and get it to move." Ryan pushed as hard as he could, but his feet slipped in the mud, and he was unable to gain traction.

Slamming the door shut, he balled his fists and resisted the urge to punch the car.

Joining Steve at the front, he put his palms on the metal hood. His heart raced with the approaching storm. He could see the line of rain coming off the mountains – it was crazy how it looked. Dust kicked up right in front of the wall of precipitation. There was a precise line separating where it was raining and what was in the path. He had seen something like that before while out on storm spotting duty, but nothing as clear and concise as what was happening just a few miles west of where they were.

Both men struggled, grunting as they fought the dark, thick soil. The car would move about an inch, and when they let up, it would slide right back to where it was. The ground was so saturated from the river rising that the chance that it would dry out anytime soon was minimal. Ryan took a deep breath, unwilling to stop. His stubborn side kicked in and he glanced at Steve, who was sweating profusely. The humidity was getting to him.

"You ready? Let's try one more damn time."

Ryan counted to three and they pushed, harder, and finally got the car up over the muddy ruts. There was some thick grass behind it, enough for the tires to gain some traction, and they finally were able to push it. Ryan kept the momentum going, but moved back to the side so he could steer it. It would be just his luck – he'd forget to maneuver it and they'd slam it right into a tree, killing their last bit of hope in having a vehicle.

"There's a grove of trees just right over there. Let's get it under that. It won't be much protection, but it'll be better than having it sit out in the open."

When they got it where they wanted, Ryan put it back in park and shut the door. They both stood to catch their breath, quiet as they tried to gain their composure. They had left their bags back near where Mrs. McElroy's body was. During the excitement of moving the car, Ryan hadn't thought about the sweet old woman.

"Moving the car was the easy part," Ryan said, glancing at Steve. "The chances of finding the tools I need are probably one in a million. But at least we got it moved."

"I didn't think we'd get it out of the mud. Looks like the storm that was coming this way sidetracked a little. Might be going south."

Ryan looked in the direction Steve was pointing and rested his hands on his hips. With low-calorie intake and so much physical work being done, he was starting to feel a dip in energy, and the day had barely started. But Steve was right – the storm was no longer coming that way. It was the break they were needing.

"We still need to watch it. With as random as everything is, it could easily swing back around and catch us off guard." Ryan patted Steve on the back. "Good work. I couldn't have done that without you."

"Just let me know what I need to do. I'm not much for working on cars or knowing what the weather is doing, but I can farm, and I can learn."

"The farming might come in handy one day if this is as bad as what I'm fearing. I'd like to think this is all a huge overreaction, but my gut is telling me the worst has yet to happen."

Ryan and Steve walked back to their supplies, both knowing they needed to do something with Mrs. McElroy. Ryan stood over her, taking his ball cap off. He had known people who had died, most peacefully, their death expected, but nothing as horrible as this. He had to tell himself that she didn't know what hit her, but the fact that she was down by the river, not close to a highway, made him think she was trying to outrun the weather. The poor woman had probably been terrified, and it killed him to think about the horrible death she had gone through.

Kneeling, he pulled the impaled wood from her midsection. It felt so undignified to have her laid out on the ground like that. They didn't have any shovels, but the ground was soft. Unfortunately, they didn't have enough time to dig a grave.

The sound of the rushing river was loud and only a few feet away. They could send her off that way, but the fear of tainting the water made that plan get shot down almost immediately. It was the only freshwater supply they had once their canteens and bottled water ran out.

"I know you knew this lady and you were close, but we can't get hung up on this, Ryan." Steve knelt beside him. "She wouldn't want you to get tied up worrying about a proper burial for her. Besides, she's not here anyway. It's just her body."

"I know," Ryan replied, feeling his voice catch in his throat. "She deserves so much better."

"She does, but you have to keep in mind that times are not how they were. We are in survival mode. Anything normal is gone, including burying the dead."

Ryan stood up and gathered some branches and greenery. Before covering her, he checked her body for anything they might be able to use. She didn't have much on her – just a few dollar bills in her pocket and a rosary. Ryan pocketed both. The money wouldn't be any good, and even though he wasn't that religious, keeping her rosary helped with the closure of just leaving her body there for wild animals and looters to mess with.

He also checked her car – she didn't have much in it either. There was a blanket in the trunk and a bag of groceries, most of it perishable and spoiling. He took the stuff that still appeared to be okay – a bag of potato chips, two brownies from her bakery, and a six-pack of Dr. Peppers. There were also a few cans of corn and green beans. The thought of the soda made his mouth water, though it probably wasn't a wise decision to drink them. The sugar rush might give them some short-term energy, but the caffeine would dehydrate them.

She had a sewing kit next to the blanket and he remembered one of her hobbies was needlework. The needles and thread might come in handy for something, so he gathered it up as well. Their load was getting heavy, but it was stuff he couldn't leave behind.

He tossed Steve the blanket. "At least you won't freeze at night anymore. I bet she crocheted that thing herself. She used to make stuff like that all the time."

"Then you keep it."

"Nah. Just carry it with us. We'll need it. And look, we've got goodies. Her brownies are amazing."

He opened the wrapper and gave one to Steve. Taking a large bite, he savored the flavor. They weren't completely fresh, but they were moist, and the chocolate icing on top was the perfect touch. The plastic wrapper had prevented any water from getting inside. It was like he was getting his first taste of sweets, and he gobbled it down in two bites.

"An ice-cold glass of milk would be perfect to wash it down," Steve said, wiping the chocolate from his chin.

"Damn straight." Ryan held up the bag of chips and the Dr. Pepper. "Looks like we got some snacks for later."

"So, what's the game plan?" Steve asked as he folded the blanket and put it in his bag.

Ryan scanned the sky. The storm was well past them, but the sky was still dark. "We need to keep going toward Harper Springs. I don't want to leave the car for too long, but right now, I need to find some tools to fix the damn thing. I'm hoping if I can get to my shop, I might come across something."

"Everything is leveled. You think there is anything left?"

"Probably not, but I'm bound to find something along the

way. Even if the buildings are gone, the stuff inside is somewhere. Might be miles from where it originated, but I've gotta try, or we moved it for nothing."

"Sounds good."

"I think we better hang back for a bit. The storm went right in the direction of Harper Springs, and I really don't want to be on the tail end of it. We'll go that way once it dissipates."

CHAPTER FIFTEEN

Darryl was growing antsy. Several days had passed and not much had changed. A few minor rainstorms had come through the area, but with him on edge and Ty stressed about his parents, every problem that came along seemed to be blown out of proportion.

Ty's health was his biggest concern. The circulation in his arm seemed to be getting worse – his skin was still blue and getting darker, and the lack of mobility made him fear that the damage would be permanent.

"How you feeling, Ty?"

He was sitting up and had just finished a can of Vienna sausages. "How come I can't feel my arm anymore?"

It had been something he had asked almost daily, and Darryl didn't know how to answer it. "I'm not sure, kiddo."

In the time between Ty sleeping and Darryl being bored out of his mind, he was able to make it easier to come in and out of the cellar. It wasn't stable and he'd never let Ty climb it by himself, but the makeshift ladder was good enough to get them in and out a lot easier than using a rope made of tree switches that would snap with repetitive use. He had finally reached the point where he knew he needed to get Ryan some sunlight. The kid had been down inside the storm shelter with no sunlight or fresh air since the whole ordeal began weeks ago.

"What do you say we get you outside for a few minutes?"

"What if another tornado comes? What if it takes me away like it took my mommy away?"

"I'll make sure to get you back down here before that happens. And I don't think a tornado took your mommy away, Ty."

Ty looked down at the floor and took a deep breath. He had done a lot of growing up, and the worry for both of his parents was obvious by all the questions he asked. Darryl didn't have the heart to tell him that the chances that he'd ever see his mom and dad were slim. Stranger things had happened, but with Ryan running around out there with not much food and nowhere to go when the weather turned, he was probably already a dead man. It killed him to think that way, and the thought of his only son being dead was painful, but they were making a new normal. The fates had shifted, and at that moment, the only thing that mattered was them staying alive and him protecting Ty.

If Ryan was dead like Darryl had feared, there would come a day when he and Ty would have to venture off to get food. He had a gun, and he could hunt. Once the bullets ran out, he could try and make a bow and arrow, which wasn't the easiest way to hunt, but an available option when the time came.

Picking Ty up, he ruffled his hair. "Let's get you some fresh air."

He slowly climbed up the wobbly ladder and swung the homemade metal door open. He pushed Ty through first and joined him at the top. The sky to the east was dark and stormy, and the humidity was so thick that you could cut a knife through it.

"Where's my house?"

It dawned on Darryl that this was the first time Ty had been outside since the very first storm. It was the first time the child had gotten a look at the way things were. A mention of his home being gone was one thing, but *seeing* it put it all into perspective, even for a boy as young as he was.

"The tornado took it, Ty. It's gone." Darryl probably could've said it better, but the truth hurt sometimes, and they were in for a lot more disappointment before it was all said and done.

"My room? My toys?"

"Everything, Grandson. I'm sorry."

Ty took a few steps forward, trying to keep his balance. He still seemed to have some vertigo, which meant whatever issues the head injury had caused were not completely gone. The fresh air would do him some good. He hoped to get him some sunlight, but it was masked by a thick blanket of dark clouds that made it feel like later in the day than it was.

"Why did the tornado take everything?"

"Because tornadoes are powerful things, Ty. One day we'll build another house and get you new toys. Everything will be fine soon."

"My mommy and daddy will be here too?"

"I sure hope so. I hope that we'll look back on all of this and it'll be nothing but a memory."

Ty moved his arm in the sling, and each time he did, Darryl saw the bone stick out from the gauze bandage. He needed to do something about it, but what? All he had on him was a knife and the first aid kit that Ryan had supplied. It didn't have much in it either – bandages, wound ointment, alcohol, and peroxide. It also had a few small packets of painkillers, which they would have to break out soon. The bottle of Tylenol and ibuprofen was running low.

Before he put Ty to bed that evening, he'd have to try and clean up the wound some more. He feared infection, and if that happened, there would be no doubt that the arm would have to be amputated to prevent it from spreading. It was either lose the arm, or Ty lose his life, and Darryl would do everything he could to not let that happen. Amputating the arm would pose other problems. It'd be an even bigger wound, which made him more vulnerable to infection. Maybe they were better off just keeping it bandaged up until he was able to get him some professional help. Without proper pain medication, the trauma alone would possibly send Ty into shock and kill him.

Darryl had to tell himself they'd cross that bridge when they got to it. Right now, it seemed fine, but what did he know? If it ain't broke, don't fix it. But it *was* broken. They needed some damn help! Maybe it was better to just take a risk and head for town. At least they'd die trying, instead of delaying the inevitable.

"Let's go walk to the trees over there. Didn't y'all used to have a barn?"

Ty nodded as if he were proud of it. He looked almost identical to Ryan at that age.

The walk was slow, and with each step they took from the cellar, it made Darryl nervous, but he couldn't hold Ty hostage underground the whole time. Getting his blood flowing might help, along with the fresh air, and hopefully, the sun if it ever decided to come out.

"We had a couple of horses, some chickens, and goats, and Daddy said we were going to get some cows!" Ty's eyes lit up when talking about the livestock.

"Cows, huh? Would you wanna get up before the sun to milk those cows?"

"I would! Grandpa, can we get some cows?"

"I don't know." He didn't know what would happen within the next hour, much less what would happen in a few weeks.

"Where are all our animals? Did the tornado take them too?"

"Maybe. Maybe the horses found a place to hide. Sometimes those are the best animals to watch whenever the weather is bad."

Ty kicked a dirt clod and watched it fall apart. "If we had a horse, we could go find my mommy and daddy!"

Darryl nodded and picked up a wrench covered in dirt. "That's a good plan, Ty! Maybe one of your horses will come back." The mention of the animals made Darryl wonder where they all were. There were plenty of horse breeders in the area, as well as cattle farmers. Was it possible that they had been completely wiped off the face of the earth? He had never heard anything like it.

"I just felt a raindrop!" Ty pointed up to the sky with his good arm.

"Which means we should probably get back to the cellar."

A rumble of thunder echoed off the mountains, making it sound bigger than it was. Since Ty still wasn't quick on his feet, Darryl worried he might trip and hurt his arm worse, so he picked him up and hurried to the shelter.

Soon, they'd have to forage for more food.

Soon, he'd have to make a decision about Ty's arm.

THE SUN WAS SETTING and Ryan still wasn't comfortable going toward Harper Springs. The weather was putting them farther behind, but the sky never cleared up and where they were seemed like the safest place. Now that it was getting dark, the best thing to do was set up camp and wait until the morning. Moving the car had taken a lot of energy, so getting some rest sounded appealing.

He gathered up more kindling and firewood. They still had plenty of matches and the lighter he carried was working. Sifting through his backpack, he pulled out their meal options. It was the same thing – beef jerky, potted meat, crackers, and the chips and Dr. Peppers that he had found in Mrs. McElroy's car. He was hungry enough to eat the options they had, but with the river close by, he wanted to try his hand at fishing.

He picked through the pile of branches and found a good sapling that would be strong enough to aid in catching a catfish. Pulling Mrs. McElroy's sewing kit out, he unwound a spool of thread and tied it to the end of the homemade pole. Making it long enough to reach the middle of the river, he bent one of the needles into the shape of a hook. It wasn't perfect, but it was better than nothing. It might not be strong enough to go through a fish, but it was worth trying.

"I never liked fishing," Steve said. "But tonight, it sounds like fun." He grabbed another sapling from the pile and rigged up the same contraption that Ryan had come up with.

"It sounds like fun and if we can get that fire going nice and big, it'll taste really nice too."

"What do you wanna use for bait?"

Ryan grabbed the can of corn and opened it with his pocketknife. "Catfish like corn and luck was on our side. Mrs. McElroy had several cans in her trunk. The thread won't be strong enough for the bigger ones, but we might be able to catch a few big enough to eat."

He threaded a kernel on the hook and sat on the edge of the river, tossing his line out as far as he could. It floated on the top of the water.

"I need to find something to weigh the line down a little," Ryan said, trying to think about what might work. "Best thing I can come up with is a small rock."

He pulled the line back in, double-checked the corn, and cut a smaller piece of thread. The rock wasn't bigger than the tip of his thumb but would weigh enough to pull it down to where the catfish would see it. Knotting the thread around it, he secured it and tossed it back in the water. This time, it sank, and hopefully, the flow of the river wouldn't make it come loose.

Though it was getting dark, it was still hot outside, so Ryan kicked his boots and socks off and dipped his feet in the water. It was cool and helped his body temperature go down. He used to love to take Ty fishing, and it made him wonder how his little guy was doing. He trusted his father with his kid, but his health was fading fast and he was starting to accept the fact that Ty would lose his arm.

"This is why I never liked fishing. I was never patient enough to wait for something to bite." Steve gave a little pull on his line.

"What else you got planned for tonight?" Ryan asked, smiling.

"I guess this is where I'm supposed to be."

Ryan felt a small tug on his line, and he pulled on it, but the corn came to the surface and there was no fish on the other end. It sank back to the bottom, and he waited.

"I'll tell you my plans," Ryan replied, sloshing his feet in the current. "I'm going to crack open an ice-cold beer, grill up some rib-eye steaks, and spend some much-needed time with my woman."

"Damn, an ice-cold beer sounds so good."

Ryan's fantasy night made his mood come crashing down. He thought about Cecilia and how much he missed her. If the storm killed her like it had Mrs. McElroy, he hoped it took her quickly.

"How long you been married?" Steve asked.

"Seven years."

"And your boy? How old is he?"

"Five." Ryan felt like he was in a trance. The mention of his dream evening probably wasn't the best idea. "I hope she's alive."

"I think I saw her, Ryan. I think she's okay."

"Yeah. For now, anyway."

"What do you mean by that?"

Ryan looked at Steve from the corner of his eye and gripped the sapling so hard that he almost broke it. "None of this is ending any time soon, that's pretty clear. If the weather doesn't get you, there's a number of other things that might. Starvation, dehydration, wild animals, and don't forget the looters running around. Why exactly were they holding you hostage? I'm still not getting that part."

"They figured the more people they got in their group, the more power they had. I guess they are wanting to start a new society where they reign over everybody."

"Then why are they killing some people?"

"I guess they're weeding out the weaker ones and the ones who don't want to comply. I wish I could make sense of it, but *nothing* makes sense."

Ryan lifted his feet out of the water and looked up at the sky. It was the first time he got a view of the stars in a long time. "As if we didn't have enough to worry about, we gotta keep an eye on being followed by those assholes too. But at least we've got that shotgun and I brought my handgun along with me. That helps ease that worry a little. But my wife likely doesn't have that. And you mention you think you saw her with a group of people. How do you know they weren't more looters who took her hostage? The guy back at the cellar seems to think that's who had her."

"I don't know that, Ryan. I'm sorry. I wish I had paid better attention, but my focus was on my situation and getting away alive."

Ryan held his hand up and chewed on the inside of his cheek. Along with a beer and a night alone with Cecilia, he would've killed for a toothbrush and a bar of soap. "No need to apologize. You didn't do a damn thing wrong."

"You'll find her, Ryan. And you'll get help for your boy."

Before Ryan could respond, a hard pull almost yanked the homemade fishing pole from his hands. He stood to get his bearings and edged it up to help prevent the weak hook from breaking and their dinner from swimming away. The catfish was bigger than he had thought the line could support, so he tried to get it up to shore as fast as he could.

The fish flopped around on the ground and the hook did pull free, but Ryan was able to grab it before it bounced back in the water to freedom. The tail slapped against his arms but there was no way in hell Ryan was going to let it get away.

"Let's get some more wood on that fire. We're going to eat well tonight!"

CHAPTER SIXTEEN

Ryan's pocketknife wasn't as sharp as the one he was used to cleaning fish with. Laying the catfish on a large rock, he ran the blade down the edge, attempting to sharpen it. Steve pulled out a bottle of propane and attached it to the lantern they were carrying, giving him more light. The fire was big but still did not produce enough light to make sure he didn't waste the fleshiest part of the fish.

He inserted the tip of the knife into the fish's underside and cut up to its head. Spreading the incision open, he removed all the fish's insides. Blood and guts squirted out, but as hungry as he was, it didn't bother him. He remembered when he tried to teach Cecilia and Ty how to clean a fish – this was the part where he always lost them, both saying it was too gross. He always had fish cleaning duties because neither of them wanted to get their hands dirty.

After making sure he had removed all the intestines and inedible pieces, he scraped his finger against the backbone, cleaning out the cavity. He rinsed it down with some water, getting the small drops of blood and things he couldn't get with his fingers. The final touch was cutting the fish head off, and he discarded all the pieces into the fire. With wild animals becoming as desperate as they were for food and water, he wanted to prevent any chance of luring them their way and becoming an easy target.

He needed a way to cook the fillets right over the open flame. They were thick pieces, and he estimated the fish was at least a ten-pounder. How it didn't break the sewing thread and fragile hook he had concocted was nothing short of a miracle. Sharpening two long sticks, the best thing they could do was hold it over the flames like a weenie roast and make sure it didn't slip off into the fire.

He handed one to Steve and began cooking their meal. The fire crackled and the smell of sizzling catfish made Ryan's stomach growl and his mouth water.

"I usually prefer catfish dipped in some cornmeal and fried up with some seasonings, but right now, I'd consider eating it raw."

"How often do you go fishing? You seem to know what you're doing." Steve rotated his fillet to the other side.

"Used to go almost every weekend. There are several lakes in the area. Never really did come to the river to do it. I wasn't even sure if I'd be able to catch anything, but looks like it's stocked up real nice with all of the rain and no one else out here fishing."

"I used to go some up in Oklahoma, but I did more bass and trout. Used to have a really nice pontoon boat and we'd have some parties right out there on Lake Canton. The drought pretty much drained that lake. It supplied Oklahoma City with its water, and last time I was up that way, it was nothing but a huge puddle. Kind of sad if you think about it."

"That's how it's been around here, too. Lake Meredith up by Amarillo was Lubbock's water supply. And it pretty much went downhill too. I've never seen this river as high as it is. I guess nature gives and takes away at the same time. But I know one thing. I'd take the drought over this any day."

Steve turned his fillet again. "Really makes you think about all that global warming stuff that has been in the news so much lately. I used to just halfway listen, not taking it seriously, but how can we explain the caliber of storms that are happening now?"

The last thing Ryan ever wanted to talk about was global warming and climate change. Weather always had fascinated him, but he had seen enough severe storms to last for three more lifetimes. What he'd give for a calm day at his house.

"I think that the earth cycles, Steve. The weather patterns change. We have the El Nino and the La Nina. El Nino makes for a more active storm season in our area. La Nina means a drier winter. That all depends on where you live. Up north, the El Nino means a milder winter." He pulled his fillet from the fire and blew on it. It was steaming and the meat was flaky, just how he liked it. He'd give it a few minutes to cool off, and then he would devour it.

"So, I guess we're in an El Nino pattern?" Steve asked.

"We were about a month ago. Hell, now, I think we're just in an apocalyptic pattern." Ryan laughed, but it wasn't that funny. It was too realistic. "Weather has gone from extreme patterns to drought for years, but the difference in this is that it's never crippled like us for weeks. I've seen tornadoes before, but the damage from them was hit-and-miss. A house gone here, a car damaged there. But everything for miles has been leveled. And where is everyone?"

"That's all things I've been wondering about too."

Ryan took a bite of the fish, and though it wasn't how he normally prepared it, it was the best thing he had tasted in a long time. It beat the hell out of potted meat and preservative-filled food he had been surviving on. And the most important thing was that it was filled with protein. It was replenishing the loss of vitamins and nutrients from his days on processed, nonperishable items.

"Any other time and I'd say this was too fishy to eat, but tonight, I wish there were seconds," Steve said as he finished his off. "Save the sapling and I can try and snag us one for breakfast. It'll be a great way to start the day."

"Definitely." Ryan glanced at the Dr. Peppers supplied by Mrs. McElroy. He'd save drinking one for in the morning as well. It'd be a nice, caffeinated boost and the sugar would help with energy too. "I plan to cover a lot of ground tomorrow, so we're going to need to get some rest tonight. I'd like to get to Harper Springs and see what the situation is there. Hopefully, we'll run across more people that I know."

Ryan smoothed out a place close to the fire and laid back on the grass. The ground was still moist and soft from all the rain, and his aching body relaxed into it. He looked up at the stars, wondering if Cecilia was seeing the same, beautiful night sky that he was. There were no clouds, and the moon was big and bright enough to give them enough light to see the river.

Coyotes howled in the distance, sounding like an old ghost in a scary movie. Ryan shivered at the thought, hoping they'd stay far enough away to not pose a threat. The scent of cooking fish would probably work against them, but the presence of human life might deter the wild dogs. Or, with food seeming scarce for everyone, they might be on their way. Being close to the river had its advantages and disadvantages.

Ryan sat up and grabbed another thick stick from the spot where he found his fishing pole. He had the shotgun and his handgun, but he wanted to make other tools and weapons to prevent using all their ammunition. Carving the tip, he downsized it to an inch in diameter and made a split-tip spear. Sharpening the edges as best as he could, he tapped his finger to test the sharpness, making sure it could puncture its target.

He made another for Steve, who had fallen asleep. He seemed to be more comfortable now that he had a blanket to keep warm, and Ryan was glad he was getting some much needed rest. He claimed his career had been farming, but so far, it didn't seem like that was the whole story. His survival skills were lacking, but Ryan wasn't an expert either. He was learning as he went, trying to use his common sense to their advantage. So far, it had worked, but it was more luck than him knowing what he was doing. Steve was quiet, but the human contact made it so that Ryan wasn't going crazy. Without someone to talk to, he'd lose his mind.

One benefit Ryan had over Steve was that he knew the land and he knew the area. He had grown up in this part of Texas, knowing that you had to respect the land and weather to be successful. Steve was from Oklahoma where the situation was similar, but it all had to be disorienting. Being in a new place, in a situation, would make anyone feel lost and confused.

With the sound of coyotes not far away, Ryan couldn't sleep. Leaning back against a tree, he held onto the spear. With the lack of human beings around, he also wondered where all the animals were. The land was spread with cattle and horses, and aside from a few dead carcasses, there had been no sign of them. He could use a horse. He wouldn't have to worry about fixing Mrs. McElroy's car if he came across one, but they had been wiped off the face of the earth like everything else.

Leaning his head back, he began to doze. The catfish was heavy in his stomach and since he wasn't hungry, he was able to get to sleep faster.

And then he heard the growling. Jolting awake, he wasn't sure how long he had been sleeping when he saw the coyote only a few feet from him, his fangs large, foam dripping from the corners of his mouth. He was ugly and ready to pounce at any second.

The spear wouldn't do Ryan any good. The animal was rabid, his eyes red and filled with anger, his body skinny from lack of food. His handgun was in his pocket and the shotgun was propped up beside him. If he made a sudden move, the wild dog would be right on top of him, and he'd never stand a chance.

Ryan moved slowly, as if he was dealing with a rattlesnake. Never taking his eyes off the coyote, he grabbed the shotgun. The dog was still growling, on the verge of making his move, ready to take a large bite out of Ryan. Steve was now awake too, and thankfully, knew not to do anything crazy. Ryan could see him from the corner of his eye, his eyes wide as they were being controlled by a mid-size beast who was diseased and ready to kill.

If he waited much longer, the coyote's patience would be gone. Pulling the shotgun in aim, the dog ran at him, and Ryan fired a shot into the night air, unable to pinpoint exactly where he wanted to aim. The animal fell to the ground, whimpering as it hit with a hard thud. If Ryan hadn't shot when he did, he'd be a dead man.

Standing, he paced around the coyote, his adrenaline pumping. It took him a second to comprehend what had happened, and when he looked over at Steve, he tried to come down off the natural high.

"Don't they usually travel in packs?" Steve asked, joining him over the motionless animal.

"Not usually. Maybe in pairs, but I've never seen a lot together. This one was sick. He had rabies." Ryan pointed down at it with his shotgun. "Holy shit, if he was rabid, that means there are others out there who are too. We've gotta be extra careful. There's coyotes, foxes, and we've even got mountain lions that come down from time to time. They're going to start looking for food, and the food chain has shifted."

"We're no longer at the top of it," Steve said, clarifying what Ryan meant.

"Yep. And the ammunition won't last forever. I made a couple of spears so we can avoid shooting if the situation allows, but if we're talking rabid animals, we're going to need stronger weapons."

"And let's not forget about the looters."

"Animals and looters," Ryan repeated, shaking his head. "I wish this nightmare would finally end." He took another long glance at the coyote. "I guess for the rest of the night, we'll need to take watch. You want first or second shift?"

Steve took the shotgun from Ryan. "I'll go first. I've already gotten some sleep. Looks like you could use some shut-eye."

"Wake me up in two hours." It was a moot point. Ryan wouldn't get a good night's rest until his family was back together, safe under one roof. Until then, insomnia was his best friend.

Leaning back against a tree on the other side of their campsite, he closed his eyes, but all he could see was the rabid coyote lunging at him, followed by the loud gun blast that saved his life. Regardless of how much rest he got, they had to push through and keep moving as soon as the sun came up.

For Cecilia, for Ty, for the looters, and to keep the animals from trailing them.

CHAPTER SEVENTEEN

As expected, Ryan hadn't slept a wink. He lay on the ground, staring up at the stars and the bright moon, and when his two hours were up, he stood guard the rest of the night, letting Steve get some rest. A few other coyotes were spotted in the distance, but they never got close enough to pose a problem.

He pulled his handgun from his pocket and slipped the magazine from the handle. It was full, but it was all he had. At least the shotgun could be used as a weapon without shells. It would just require getting closer to whatever nuisance was causing problems, whether it was another person or rabid dogs. He had left some of the ammunition and guns acquired from the looters with his father so they had some protection.

The sun slowly came up over the top of the mountains. There wasn't a cloud in the sky, and for a moment, Ryan hoped that the weather would be perfect to cover several miles. He had a hard time getting a good vantage point, but Harper Springs was still probably a good seven to eight miles north of their location. If everything cooperated, they could get there later in the day if they kept a good pace. Having a decent dinner the night before was helpful, he just wished he was able to get more sleep.

He gathered up some pine needles for kindling, stacked some wood, and got a fire going. Coffee sounded good, and he poured some water and grounds into the percolator. It was becoming their biggest necessity. It'd be his saving grace after a crazy night. With so many people relying on him, he had to be smart. If only he could reach his dad on his cell phone and see how Ty was doing, that would ease a fraction of his stress.

Steve stretched out and tossed the blanket aside, grumbling something about how early it was. "What's for breakfast?"

"Bacon, eggs, and hash browns," Ryan replied, smirking. It made his mouth water, and he pulled a package of pop tarts from his bag, compliments of the looters. They were brown sugar and cinnamon, and would taste great with the coffee.

Tossing Steve a foil pack, he opened his and dipped it in his drink. He looked over at the dead coyote he had shot just hours before. Too bad it wasn't edible.

"Bacon and eggs sound amazing," Steve said as he poured himself a mug of coffee. "How low are we running on this?"

"Half a bag. I guess we better cut down and not have it every morning."

"You look exhausted, Ryan. Are you okay?"

"Couldn't sleep." Ryan shrugged and stoked the fire. "You see anything when you were on lookout last night?"

"Not a damn thing. I know you care about that woman over there," Steve pointed over his shoulder toward Ms. McElroy, "but I think the body is gonna start attracting more wild animals."

"I'm planning to head north after we finish with breakfast. By the time we get back to fix the car, her body will likely be gone anyway. You're right, I do care for her, but she's gone. I have to wonder how many more folks we'll run across that I know."

Steve didn't say anything, and Ryan gathered up their supplies. Sloshing the propane bottle, they still had a good supply of it. He looked over the car one last time, assessing the damage. By the time they got back, maybe it'd be completely dry, but interior damage was already occurring. Maybe he'd find what he'd need on the way to town. But having a car would solve a lot of problems. He could drive his family out of here and to a place of safety, where the weather hadn't destroyed everything. Did a place like that even exist anymore? He'd never know until they could be mobile and leave.

"We'll follow the highway today. I think we might have a better chance of running across others, and maybe find a functional car. We can zig-zag toward the river if we are running low on food or water, but if we move fast, that won't matter. If you have any ideas on anything, let me know. But we gotta get going." He tossed Steve's bag to him and gathered their supplies.

"There's not a cloud in the sky. It's nice to see some blue for a change."

There was a dusty haze at eye level, but it was pretty. "All the more reason for us to keep going. A clear morning is a huge ingredient for an active afternoon. I know of a few farms between here and where we are going, so if need be, we might have a cellar to get to just in case."

"And in town? Are there storm shelters?"

Ryan nodded and sipped from the canteen. "There's a community cellar and a few of the churches have basements. Lots of the houses do too. That's where we might be able to find more supplies. People use them as storage rooms, and if they haven't already been ravaged, it'll feel like a gold mine."

He took one last look at Mrs. McElroy, the reality finally setting in that the casualties were outnumbering the living. Weaving down a trail, Ryan was satisfied with the immediate boost of energy. A combination of coffee, a good dinner, and a game plan made him feel inspired. He tried not to think about the past. He was going to get help and find Cecilia, come hell or high water, and luckily for them, he was already enduring both.

DARRYL SPENT most of his time walking around, seeing what he could find out in the pasture. He had gathered up a pile of junk with no plan on what the items could be used for. He had gotten Ty out of the cellar, spending a little more time each day in the fresh air, but making sure he took it easy. The boy seemed dizzy and confused at times, and since he claimed he couldn't feel his arm, he was moving it around more, which Darryl feared would cause even more damage.

What would Ryan do in this situation? There was a small infection right near the bone, but it didn't appear to be spreading yet. He didn't know where to begin when it came to amputation. What would be worse? Taking the arm or allowing the infection to grow? He was damned if he did and damned if he didn't.

"So, what all do we have, Grandpa?" Ty stood over the pile of things. It was like a scavenger hunt for the little guy, and it was getting both of their minds off everything else.

They both sat beside the pile, sifting through it. "Well, there's a hammer, a wrench, a leather strap, probably for the horses, and a hairbrush." Darryl held it up and ran it through Ty's hair. It was starting to get shaggy, and he scrubbed his hand down his face. His beard was full now and he probably looked like a mountain man.

"That looks like my mommy's!" Ty's eyes lit up. "She will want that!"

Darryl nodded and looked away. Oh, to have the innocence of a child. Ty wasn't stupid, but wasn't aware about the severity of their situation. Ryan and Cecilia were gone. He wasn't sure if they'd ever make it back or be reunited. And Ty was staring down at the junk pile in awe. At least it was fun for him, and he wasn't depressed and stuck down in the cellar all day.

Darryl glanced up from their stack of debris, and his heart skipped a beat. A man he didn't recognize stood at the opening of the cellar, peering inside. He was covered in dirt and grime and looked up to no good. Darryl remained cautious - times like this brought desperation out in some of the most honest people.

Darryl stood between him and the boy. There were about forty yards between them. "Mister, can I help you with something?"

"No. You can't help me with a damn thing."

"What can I do for you?"

"The man who lives here. Where is he?"

Darryl looked down at Ty, who watched on like it was a movie playing out on the big screen. How did he know Ryan, and what did he want with him?

"He's not here."

"I can see that! Where is he?"

Darryl tried not to make any sudden movements. He didn't know if the man was armed or what he might be capable of. "He went to get some help. He's trying to find his wife."

"Everyone is dead. He'll be dead soon too. Both of you will be, too."

"Everything will work out, Mister."

"Stop calling me mister! My name is Doug, and I'm looking for the man who lives here! He killed my brother, and he locked me in a cellar!"

Did Ryan really do that? Maybe he had the person mixed up. How did he know Ryan even lived here? "Are you sure you're at the right place? That doesn't sound like something my son would do."

"So, he's your son, huh?" Doug's eyes widened and he looked down at Ty. "So that makes that little kid *his* son? I ought to shoot him like he shot my brother! I should take away something of his since he took something of mine!"

Darryl was aware of the gun in his pocket. It was just a small, twenty-two caliber pistol, but if he needed to use it, it'd at least slow Doug down. He wouldn't allow anything to happen to Ty.

"I'm going to ask you again, Doug. How do you know that the guy who did that to your brother lives here?"

"We came by a few weeks ago. It was him! He chased us off. And now I'm back to finish it all off."

"Why did he kill your brother? Ryan isn't a killer. There must have been a reason."

Doug shook his head and tears rolled down his cheeks. "That doesn't matter. None of this matters. We will all be dead soon. If your son is out there right now, he won't make it back. But at least I'll have the satisfaction of knowing I got revenge for my brother!" He pounded his chest with his fist and spit escaped from the corner of his mouth. "I can't let him die in vain!"

"And you're not going to kill a kid," Darryl said, staying between Ty and Doug. "I know you're desperate. We all are. Going around looting and wreaking havoc is only going to make it worse. Coming together and being a team is what will make us overcome all of this." Darryl spread his hands, motioning toward their surroundings. "I'd say sorry for Ryan killing your brother, but I'm sure he did it for a reason. My best guess is he did it because you were about to kill him, yeah?"

"He was a threat to our plan."

"And what plan might that be? World domination? You saw a chance to take control and Ryan was going to mess it up, is that it?"

"We figured if we got the upper hand, the strong would survive. We didn't want to be weak. We wanted to survive!" He pounded his chest again. "And now my brother is gone, and I have no one."

"I don't know, but I bet there's some good in that heart. Help is coming. Don't you want to be on the right side of the law when things get back to normal?"

"Normal? What does that word even mean? The life you knew before is gone. This is how it is. Ain't no one gonna give a damn about the law. All that matters is who is strong and who can survive. Killing my brother knocked me down for a bit, but I found a way out of that cellar and here I am. I am a thorn in your son's side. He will *not* become the leader. It'll be me! Taking something near and dear to him will knock him off his high horse, and that is why I'm here! If it can't be him that I kill, at least I can get the next best thing."

Doug looked at Ty and took several steps forward. Darryl pulled the pistol from his pocket and aimed. If he hesitated too long, it'd be too late, and Ty would be gone. Just as he swore to Ryan, he wouldn't let anything happen to the kid. He aimed low and pulled the trigger. A loud shot echoed, and Doug fell to the ground, his face in the mud below.

"Grandpa, you shot him!"

It wasn't a life-threatening wound, but one that slowed him down. Rolling on his back, Doug let out a yell and held his leg. Darryl had hit him in the shin, and a small spot of blood soaked into his pants.

Standing over him, Darryl aimed the gun between Doug's eyes. "You come any closer to my grandson, and I'll make sure this one kills you." At point-blank range, even the twenty-two was strong enough to finish the job.

Doug crawled away, leaving a blood trail in the dirt. It didn't seem that serious, but with the lack of healthcare and emergency personnel, it could pose a problem. He put his hands over the wound and refused to make eye contact with Darryl.

"I don't have enough food to support you here, but I'm going to make damn sure you don't go hurt anyone else, you get me?" Darryl knelt beside him and offered a piece of gauze. "It's going to hurt for a while, but you'll live. You better be glad I didn't have a bigger gun on me."

"If you expect me to say thank you, you're mistaken," Doug said through clenched teeth. "Your son left me some food when he locked me in the cellar. I put some in my bag over there." He pointed to the duffel bag by the cellar door.

"I told you he wasn't a killer. Ryan's a good guy."

"I don't share the same opinion. So, what now?"

"I mean what I say. You're not going to go hurt anyone else. And from the looks of things, you won't be walking that far for a while." Darryl grabbed some of the rope Ryan had made and secured Doug to a tree. "There's only a few men I trust in this world, and you ain't one of them. With my grandson being threatened, I've gotta keep you tied up."

He checked the knots. They weren't the strongest, so he'd have to keep an eye on him. They'd serve as decent restraints temporarily, but Darryl wouldn't be surprised if Doug managed to break loose. He patted him down, pulling a knife from his pocket. Past that, he didn't have anything useful on him.

"You really think I could hurt a child?" Doug asked, glaring up at him.

"I don't know what to think. I don't know you. But you came here with a plan to hurt Ryan, and that is enough evidence for me to know that you're capable of just about anything. I'd rather not take a chance."

"And what if a storm comes? I'll die tied up to a tree like this!"

"I guess you should've thought about that before you decided to go mess with people." Darryl turned his attention back to Ty. "Hey buddy, let's get the stuff you found gathered up. It's time to eat."

CHAPTER EIGHTEEN

The sound of silence was deafening. Ryan and Steve were quiet for most of the day, but one thing that bugged Ryan was the calm weather. Daytime temperatures easily climbed almost to 100, but the sky was as blue as a normal day. It felt weird to complain about something like that. It was allowing them to cover several miles without having to outrun shards of hail and lightning. He didn't dare say anything out loud and chance jinxing it, but it wasn't normal.

There wasn't a single abandoned car or sign of life for miles. Ryan used the spear he made as a walking stick and adjusted the strap on the shotgun. As they gathered supplies, their load was getting heavy, but he wasn't willing to part with any of it, even if it was something as simple as a screw or nail.

Jabbing the point into the mud, he pushed harder with each step. It was a good stress relief, and it kept his mind from running in a million different directions. The sun beat down on them and he licked his lips, but no moisture was left on his tongue. He drank from the canteen and offered some to Steve, who took a long pull. It wasn't cold anymore, but at least it was wet. He was getting dehydrated, but until they went back toward the river, it would have to do.

"I never thought I'd say this, but I wish it'd rain. Nothing crazy, just a nice rain shower to cool us down some."

"Look over there!" Steve pointed to the west. It was an old farmhouse, half-way standing. It was the only structure Ryan had seen that hadn't been completely swept away. It wasn't livable, but two of the four walls were still intact. Maybe someone would be there.

Hurrying his pace, Ryan jogged toward it, yelling out. No one answered and as he got closer, he realized it was one of his customers. Taking his cap off, he felt the emotions well up inside him.

"Larry?"

"You know who lives here?"

Ryan nodded and stumbled up the rickety steps. The roof was caved in, and bricks had toppled over in large piles. A tree cascaded over what was left. If he was ready to stop for the night, it would've served as the perfect shelter.

"He was one of my frequent fliers. He had several old trucks he used on his farm." And as luck would have it, there wasn't a single truck left. How could a storm be so random in its destruction?

"He have a cellar?"

"No, I think this house had a basement."

Ryan was careful where he took his steps. A nail through the sole of his boot would be painful. Broken glass crackled under his feet, and in the middle of the wreckage laid an old picture of Larry and his wife. Picking it up, Ryan wiped the frame with his index finger. Droplets of condensation were inside the glass, but the picture seemed to be okay.

"That's him. His wife died a couple of years ago. Car wreck. Ever since then, he spent a lot of time at the shop. He always wanted someone to talk to, and I didn't mind the conversation."

"Maybe he's in his basement waiting for someone to come get him."

Ryan dug through the mess. He never visited Larry at his

house, but he found an opening on the floor that revealed a big staircase. It was pitch black and he flipped on a flashlight as he went down.

"Larry!"

There was no response, and when Ryan reached the floor, he flashed the light beam in every corner, stopping when he saw something crouched on the ground. Approaching slowly, he remained cautious. With all the looters and uncertainty, he didn't want to walk right into a trap.

"Larry?" He pushed on the man's shoulder, and the body fell to the floor. It was Larry, and he was dead. Ryan took a step back, his breath catching in his throat. "Son of a..."

Steve joined him. "Holy shit!"

"Doesn't seem to be any foul play. Probably died of thirst." Now wasn't the time to get caught up in another person's death. Before everything was said and done, he'd probably run across more than he was willing to count. Right then, it was time to search for things they could use. "He liked tinkering with cars. Maybe he's got some tools."

Ryan and Steve searched. There wasn't much in the basement, only some canned food that looked to have been several years old. He'd make a mental note of it in case they had to come back, but they couldn't carry it all.

"I didn't find anything, Ryan."

"Me either. I bet he kept all his stuff out at his shop, which was behind the house." A sense of dread hit Ryan. "Son of a bitch!" He kicked a cabinet and the canned food rattled. "It's like fate wants us to die!" Gritting his teeth, he checked Larry for anything useful. He hated how easy it was becoming. The fact that he didn't have to hesitate to comb his dead friend's body over for supplies put a whole new perspective on the situation. This was what normal now was. No one was coming. It wasn't a game, and they weren't on a reality show. This was *life*.

Taking Larry's boots off, Ryan tossed them to Steve. "We'll eventually wear ours out. Keep these as backups."

Larry had a screwdriver and a crescent wrench in his pocket, and he added them to his backpack. He also stripped him of his clothes – a flannel shirt, a tank top, and a good pair of jeans. He also took his baseball cap and his gold necklace. The hoarder mentality was what Ryan believed would help keep them alive.

"He's about our size. We can use this stuff if we need to."

Steve folded the clothes and they went back up the stairs. They were surprised to see a rain shower blowing through. The tree draped over the house looked like a beautiful waterfall in someone's garden, and Ryan held the canteen under a group of leaves, allowing the water to run into his canteen.

It was a steady enough stream to completely refill it, and once his was full, he did the same for Steve's. The rain cooled the temperature down about twenty degrees, and for the first time, it made Ryan feel rejuvenated. Once the canteens were refilled, he dipped his head under the leaves, the freshwater falling right into his mouth, killing the sandpaper thickness on his tongue. Water never tasted so good, and Steve followed suit, finding a spot where the rain trickled down for him to get a taste.

Something so small changed Ryan's mood. As soon as the rain started, it stopped, but it was a refreshing change from the hail, lightning, and suctioning winds. After they were satisfied with searching through the remains of the house, they kept going. Ryan glanced at his watch. It was after two PM, and they were covering a lot of ground.

"Larry's house is about three miles from Harper Springs. If we keep going, we'll reach town before the sun goes down. How you feeling?"

Steve wiped the sweat from his brow and put Larry's ball cap on. His skin was red from the sun and Ryan didn't realize that sunburns would eventually pose a problem for them too.

"A little hungry, but let's keep going."

Ryan tossed him the bag of beef jerky. They were running low, but it was the most protein-filled thing they had. He'd have a small piece and hope that would hold them over. Reaching town might give them a plethora of rubble to sift through, or it could come up as a dead end like everything else, but it was the only thing he had to look forward to. It'd also give them a better chance of running into Dr. Robbins or the nurses who worked in his office. He could tell them about Ty's situation, and they could give him some medical advice on how he could help the child.

Maybe Cecilia would be there. The fact that he hadn't run across her car along the highway gave him hope that she had gotten there before the storm came crashing in. That *had* to be what happened. He couldn't accept any other possibility, or all of this was for nothing.

They continued to walk, and with their canteens full, they wouldn't have to sidetrack back to the river to get more water. As before, there was a big, dark storm in the sky just to the north of them, so Ryan kept close watch. It was working in their favor for the time being – the temperatures off the back side kept things cool, which meant that the storm was loaded with hail. It was likely hitting Fox Lake, which is where Cecilia's parents were. He often wondered about their safety, but he had to keep his goals small without feeling too overwhelmed.

He felt like their pace was lagging, and when he looked back at Steve, another worry developed. His traveling partner was looking red and tired, and his feet were dragging. Ryan motioned toward the canteen around his neck.

"Get some more to drink."

"I don't want to run out."

"We can go back to the river if we have to. You need to drink. You don't look so good."

Steve didn't put up much of a fight and took a long pull, wiping his mouth with the back of his hand. What natural remedies could they use for sunscreen? Steve looked like he was getting burned up fast, which was odd because Ryan didn't seem to be burning as bad. Ryan was also darker complected compared to the fair-skinned man, and it was taking its toll on him.

Finding a spot to stop, Ryan took the tank top he had found

on Larry and cut the lower part off. Pouring water on the cloth, he lifted Steve's hat and put it underneath, allowing some of it to fall on his neck.

"Your own little air conditioner."

"It takes too much water, Ryan. I'm fine."

"We need to get back to the river so you can cool off."

Steve looked over his shoulder. "How far is it? That will set us back too much."

"I could use a dip myself. The river makes a turn a little up the highway. There's a bridge we cross over about a half a mile up. Rattlesnake Bridge is the name of it. Maybe I can spear us a snake to have for dinner."

"Or we get bit by one. I don't want to hold you back, Ryan. I know you're in a hurry to get to Harper Springs."

"What good will we be if we dehydrate ourselves? It's a small setback, but a good one. Rehydrate, try to catch a fish or a snake, and recharge ourselves. I won't be any use to my wife if I die out here because we got dehydrated and burned up. Besides, that storm just north of here looks like it's stationary. If we take our time, it'll give it a chance to dissipate or move on before we come up right underneath it."

Steve didn't put up any more of an argument and Ryan led him in the direction of Rattlesnake Bridge. He wasn't sure why it was named that. He had fished off the bridge several times and never saw one, but now would be a good time to see one, if he could keep his distance and kill it before it struck at them.

Steve was slower than just a few minutes before, and when they reached the river, Ryan stripped down to his undershirt and boxers, diving into the cool water. The mud between his toes felt good, and wiping the dirt all over his skin made him feel like a new man. Steve edged his way in, ducking his head under the surface. Ryan scrubbed his fingers through his hair and his beard – it was thick now, and though it seemed that it would make him hot, it was keeping him cool. It was also helping block his skin from the sun. He hadn't had facial hair this long since right after graduating high school.

He took a second to watch Steve. The poor guy looked as red as a lobster. His facial hair was coming in blond and not quite as thick as Ryan's. What could they do to make some natural sunblock? Ryan wished he would've paid more attention in science class. Aloe Vera was perfect for soothing burning skin, but that didn't help block the UV rays.

After another five minutes of enjoying the cool water, Ryan got out and put his clothes back on. Sitting on the edge of the water, he pulled his sapling from his supplies and rigged up another hook from Mrs. McElroy's sewing kit. Stabbing a piece of corn on the end, he tossed the line in the river and waited. Steve was enjoying the water downstream, and it was good to see him smiling again.

Ryan ran his hand through the mud just under the surface of the water. That was it! Steve could put some on his skin. It would help block the rays. Balling a glob in his fist, Ryan held it up and yelled toward Steve.

"When you get out, put some of this on your exposed skin!"

Steve cocked his head to the side. "Right after a cleansing bath?"

"It'll help with the sunburn. A little on your face, the back of your neck, and your arms. I'm going to do it too. Probably would be best to prevent blistering."

"I never would've thought of that," Steve replied, shaking his head as he dove back under the water.

Ryan turned back to fishing, feeling a small tug on the line from the flow of the river. For a moment, he was able to remove himself from the situation. At that second, he was just a man, fishing on the banks of the river, hoping to snag dinner. He was able to imagine that the world around him wasn't in utter chaos, and that things were fine. Cecilia was back home, preparing the rest of the meal, and Ty was healthy, running freely out in the pasture.

The growling behind him pulled him from his dream world. What in the hell was it? He was afraid to turn and look. Glancing over his shoulder, he dropped the sapling and got a look at the coyote that was about twenty yards from him. Steve was in the river, unarmed, unable to shoot from where he was. Ryan had the handgun in his pocket, but the angle was bad, and he wouldn't be able to get it out without making a sudden movement that would trigger the dog's reflexes and come after him.

He got up slowly, his heart thumping so hard that it was about to fall out of his chest. The dog showed his teeth, the large fangs ready to bite right into his skin. There was no foam dripping from his mouth like the one from the night before, but all bets were off now. As Steve had said, humans were no longer at the top of the food chain. Wildlife was getting hungry, and they were willing to go after anything to survive. The fact that the coyote was out during the day was worrisome.

Behind Ryan was the river. He could jump back in and make the coyote swim after him. How good of swimmers were they? Didn't rabid animals fear water? He thought he had read that somewhere.

If he yelled for Steve, that would be another reason to give the coyote a chance to lunge. Taking a deep breath, Ryan moved his left foot back, and that was enough for the coyote to come after him.

Everything felt like it was moving in slow motion. Instead of falling back into the river, Ryan moved to the side, trying to make a far circle around the animal, but its reflexes were quick, and it nipped at his heels as he tried to run for a tree. He could feel the hot breath off the coyote, his teeth clamping down and snapping, barely missing Ryan by a few inches. The gun was heavy in his pocket, but if he tried to pull it out, that would also slow him down. But he had to try! He couldn't just let the coyote have him for a meal.

He sprinted as fast as he could, but the uneven terrain made it hard to run full speed. If he looked back, it'd slow him down, but the wild dog was right there. He slid his hand into his pants pocket, but it didn't work. The gun was too big to pull out and he'd have to stop to be able to get it. He tripped on something, his body crashing hard to the ground. Sharp pain and heat shot through him, and his head slammed into the earth below, the edge of his vision growing fuzzy.

A loud gunshot exploded from above – it was the last thing Ryan heard before passing out.

CHAPTER NINETEEN

"Ryan? Ryan, are you okay?"

He could hear someone's voice, distant like he was in a tunnel. He tried to get up, but his body screamed out in pain, and he fell back against whatever it was he was lying on. It took a second for his vision to recover from the blurriness, and he finally saw Steve hovering over him like a helicopter circling a suspect.

"Oh, thank God, you're awake!"

Ryan lifted his head, but it felt like it weighed 100 pounds. "What the hell?"

"You don't remember?"

"Enlighten me, please. I can only imagine." The sound of his own voice made Ryan's head hurt, and he cringed with each pulse that made his brain want to explode against his skull.

"You got attacked by a coyote."

"I what?" Was it a damn dream? The pain in his leg said otherwise, and he finally got enough energy to sit up and see his pants were ripped and there was a piece of cloth wrapped around his thigh, pink from the blood it was absorbing. "What the hell?" he asked again, unable to think up a coherent question.

"The coyote didn't do that. You fell on a metal fence post."

Ryan went to remove the bandage, but Steve stopped him, his grasp hard on his hand. "I wouldn't remove it just yet. It's still bleeding, and this isn't exactly the most sanitary place to have an open wound."

"What did you wrap it in?"

"The rest of Larry's tank top."

That wasn't sanitary either, but at it was better than nothing.

"I want to see it. How deep is it?"

"It could use stitches."

"Shit!" Ryan laid his head back again and closed his eyes. "You're worried about sanitation, and I impaled my leg on a rusty metal pole." Things like tetanus popped into his mind, and he rubbed his finger down his cheek, thinking about lockjaw. "Is it bad enough that I won't be able to walk?"

"Probably not for a few days. I cleaned it with some of the alcohol we had in the first aid kit. I'm surprised that didn't wake you up. It foamed up and seemed to do a good job. I bet it burned like crazy."

"I don't have a few days. We have to keep going." He sat up again, adjusting his weight.

"This is my fault, Ryan." Steve sat beside him. "We should've never stopped. You would've never gotten attacked and hurt. And we'd probably already be in Harper Springs by now."

"No, don't do this." Ryan wagged his index finger at Steve. "You weren't in good shape yourself. It was my idea to stop. We aren't going to play the blame game, you got me? If we do that, we should blame it all on mother nature and the bitch she's been!"

He felt lightheaded and out of breath. It was like something was working against them – like they shouldn't be out there. They should be dead, like everyone else. Maybe it would have been better if he allowed the storm to take them, so they weren't left behind to go through all the suffering and struggles. He couldn't let himself think that way. The brain believes what you tell it, and all of it would be in vain if he allowed a pessimistic attitude ruin everything.

"We need to find a doctor," Steve said, stating the obvious.

Ryan clenched his jaw and stared down at his wounded leg. "Thank you, Steve. You saved my life. Which gun did you use?"

"The shotgun. It was propped up against a tree. I jumped out of the water as soon as I saw the damn thing bearing down on you. You're a fast runner! He damn near got a piece of you!"

Ryan couldn't help but laugh. "At first, I didn't think you realized what was going on, but my focus was on the animal. That's quick thinking. I'd be dead..."

Steve's brow furrowed and he looked away. "But you're not. And you'd do the same for me, so don't think that way."

Ryan bit his bottom lip to stave off a bout of pain that shot through him. "I've gotta worry about tetanus or other infections. So along with finding my wife, getting medical help for my son, and getting tools to fix that car, we've gotta run across a tetanus shot, somehow."

"When was the last time you had the shot?"

"Hell, I don't know. Long enough to where I'll need one. Maybe you ought to find your own way. I seem to be a magnet for attracting all kinds of bullshit. I'm an accident just waiting to happen."

"You've gotten us this far, Ryan. We're not far from Harper Springs and we'll keep moving. But you need to rest and stay off that leg for a while. If you don't, you'll just hurt yourself worse."

"So close, yet so far," Ryan replied. When was he going to wake up from this nightmare?

"That storm we were waiting on near Harper Springs looks like it finally moved off." Steve handed Ryan a canteen and a bottle of Tylenol. "Probably should take a few of those."

Ryan didn't argue. The water tasted good, and it was cold, and he swallowed four pills. "How bad is the wound? I know I already asked that, but did it go through?"

"No." Steve shook his head. "It's a pretty big gash and it's deep. It's going to leave a hell of a scar. By my calculations, it won't get stitched up in time to prevent one. Unless!" He snapped his fingers, his eyes widening as the idea hit him.

"Unless what?" Finally, Steve was showing some personality, and it threw Ryan off guard.

"We have that woman's sewing kit, right?"

Ryan looked down at his leg. The cotton shirt was soaked in his blood, and it didn't show any signs of slowing down. "You're wanting to stitch me up?" His heart skipped a beat. "That has infection written all over it. Do you even know how to do it?"

"I've got livestock. I've had to do it to them when the veterinarian wasn't around. And there is a risk for infection, but so is leaving the wound wide open with dirty bandages and your soiled clothes over it. We've got the rubbing alcohol I can pour on it. It'll hurt like hell, but we gotta get it to stop bleeding."

Ryan shifted his weight, trying to lift the leg. He could barely get it off the ground without the pain shooting through him, hindering any chance of moving. And he felt weak – likely from blood loss and malnutrition.

"If you don't want me to do it, I won't touch you. If it were me, I'd do it. Look how much blood has soaked into your jeans." He pointed at Ryan's leg. "I'm no doctor, but like I said, I've stitched up cattle before. You'll definitely have a scar, but I think that's a moot point right about now."

It *would* hurt like hell. Ryan contemplated the option a few more minutes, hesitating. "How long ago did this happen?" He still wasn't sure how much time had passed. If he could get an accurate timeline, it'd help him make a decision.

"You were out for a good forty-five minutes."

"And I've been awake for about fifteen, so an hour, give or take. And it's still bleeding." Ryan shook his head yes. "We can try it. I'm damned if I do and damned if I don't." He wanted to give it more time, but they didn't have any more time to waste. "The sewing kit is in the big pocket of my backpack. There are different size threads and needles. Probably should get a thicker thread."

Steve gathered the supplies and laid them out beside Ryan. He poured alcohol on a cotton ball and smoothed it down the needle, including the tip. Eying the spool, he smirked and unrolled several feet.

"We don't have flesh color, so you'll have black stitches. We're gonna have to pull your pants down so I can get better access to it. Don't want to cross-contaminate with your clothes."

Ryan edged his jeans down, thankful he still had a pair of boxers on. The fabric clung to the dried blood on his skin, and he was already anticipating the horrible pain. He wished they had something to numb him. If only his dad were there with his flask of whiskey. If he had a good buzz going, he wouldn't care what Steve did.

Steve pulled Ryan's belt through the loops and handed it to him. "I'd bite down on this. It might help a little."

Ryan let out a sarcastic laugh. It was shocking how willing Steve was to perform the procedure, as if he was his special science project. When Steve removed the gauze and cloth, Ryan got his first real look at the injury. The gash was about six inches long, and deep enough that he could see tissue. More blood oozed out, along with some pus, which wasn't a good sign. The gauze stuck to the dried blood like his jeans had, and he cringed at the sight of the injury, and the hell he was about to endure to get it sewn up.

Steve dabbed a few drops of alcohol on a clean piece of gauze and held it right above the wound. "You ready?"

"Do it. Just get it over with," Ryan said between breaths, closing his eyes when the bandage soaked in medicine ran over his skin.

Painful was an understatement. He could feel the alcohol bubbling in and around the affected area, the discomfort feeling like a million needles were jabbing into him. He bit down on his belt so hard that he almost split the leather. Sweat flowed down the side of his face and he tasted the salt on his lips. Maybe this was a mistake. Maybe he should've given it a little more time to heal up on its own.

The pain subsided for a moment, the wound going numb from the trauma. Steve set the gauze and bottle of alcohol aside and made sure the needle was clean again. Tying the thread through the eye, he secured it and looked at Ryan from the corner of his eye.

"Maybe that was the worst of it."

"You're about to stick a needle in my skin. I'm not sure what to..."

Steve didn't give him a chance to finish his sentence. Surprisingly, it didn't hurt as bad as cleaning it had, and he felt the tension pull the damaged flesh together. There was a dull ache deep in his leg, but the stinging had subsided. It felt weird, having thread weave in and out, but Ryan finally gained enough courage to open his eyes and watch. Steve was better at stitching him up than expected. He must've done it a lot on his farm.

As the needle moved in and out, a few more drops of blood seeped out, but it was a small sacrifice to make in comparison to the amount of blood he'd lose if they hadn't taken action. His skin didn't match up perfectly, but it would help aid his body in healing. He wasn't going for a beauty contest. A scar would just be a mark to remind him of the adventure they were on.

Finishing the job, Steve cinched it up and cut the remaining thread with his pocketknife, leaving about two inches for some slack. For safe measure, he ran another cotton ball soaked in alcohol over the stitches. Another sensation of pain hit Ryan, but it ended quickly.

"I should be a surgeon," Steve said, laughing. "What do you think, Ryan?"

"My leg looks like a damn football."

"And you stopped bleeding," Steve replied as he gathered up the supplies.

"Thanks, Steve. I appreciate it. I owe you."

"No, you don't. You got me away from those looters. And besides, we're not keeping score. We're in this together. I can't have you bleeding all over the damn place. The coyotes will surely track us then!"

Ryan felt a smile part his lips, and it wasn't forced. His eyelids were heavy, and he felt like he had just got done running a race. Sitting up, he fought the wave of exhaustion and drank some more water. Since they were by the river, they could easily get a refill.

"We should get going if that storm is gone."

Steve's eyes widened again as if Ryan had spoken another language. "Are you kidding me? You've got a massive hole in your leg! I just stitched it up. Your ass isn't going anywhere!"

"We don't have the time to wait around. Whether we go right now or hours from now, my leg is going to hurt. I wanted to get to Harper Springs before the sun went down today." He attempted to get up again, but this time, Steve made it impossible, gently putting his hand on Ryan's chest.

"What good will you be if you won't rest? Rushing it is just going to slow us down more. You took a detour for me to get water. Now do it for yourself, would you? You're a stubborn ass!"

Steve's assessment of Ryan made him laugh, and laughing made him hurt, but he couldn't stop himself. "My wife says the same thing about me."

"I know you wanna find her. I get it. But you can barely hold your eyes open while you're talking to me. You said so yourself before I stitched you up – you're worried about infection. Going too soon will weaken you, including your immune system."

Ryan held his hand up and bit his bottom lip. "Alright. Point made. You sure you're not a car salesman? And you say I'm the stubborn one?"

"We'll rest this evening and see how you feel in the morning. That'll give me time to fish and make supper. You need something to keep your strength up."

Ryan didn't respond. Steve knew what he was doing, and it

was nice to witness him finally coming out of his shell. As much as Ryan liked to lead, sometimes it was a nice break to follow for a change.

Waiting around posed potential problems – another storm coming through was his biggest worry, along with looters and more wild animals. He wasn't mobile, and he wouldn't be able to get away, should any of those scenarios happen. He was in a prime position to be a quick meal.

Steve carried his sapling to the edge of the water and threw it in. Another catfish would hit the spot if he was able to catch one. Ryan closed his eyes and tried to rest. One second at a time. That's all they could do.

CHAPTER TWENTY

Ryan woke up to his leg throbbing. Lifting his head off the tree, it took a second to remember what happened, but when he tried to stand, his memory came back to him, and he groaned out in pain. He looked around for Steve, not finding him. The humid air was thick on top of his chest, and he had to tell himself to breathe slowly, even though the pain in his leg was unbearable.

"Steve?" It didn't come out as loud as he anticipated. "Steve?" Had he left? Did a coyote get him? Ryan tried to stand up again, but a shadow blocked the sun bearing down on him, and he saw the silhouette of his travel buddy towering over him.

"I wouldn't get up, Ryan. Wouldn't want to bust those stitches." Steve moved to where Ryan got a better view of him, and he was holding two catfish on the end of Mrs. McElroy's thread. "Dinner tonight. They aren't big, but they'll feed us."

"Want me to clean them?"

Steve shook his head and laid them out on a flat rock. One of the fish's fins moved, but it was its last bit of life before it came to a rest next to the other.

"I want you to rest, Ryan. I can clean a fish. I'll even get the fire going. If you take it easy the rest of the day and tonight, we probably will be able to go again tomorrow. The weather has held up for now, but we are about due for something big soon. I don't think I can carry you, and if I could, we still wouldn't move fast enough."

Ryan tried to move his leg to keep the blood flow going. It felt numb like when his foot would fall asleep, and he wasn't sure if that was a good sign. When he was running from the coyote, his adrenaline was going, and he didn't even feel pain when he fell, but now that his shock was wearing off, the ache was strong. Steve offered him two ibuprofen and the canteen, and he downed the pills with a large gulp of water. It was refreshing and tasted good, so he took a few more sips before giving it back to him.

"I know I already said it, but thank you, Steve. I'd have been that coyote's dinner if it wasn't for you."

"He almost got you, but you're fine. It's no problem. Besides, I need you alive. I'd be lost out here. Probably already dead."

Ryan lifted his injured leg a few inches off the ground and cringed, but he had to keep moving it. His dad had gotten a knee replacement a year ago and the first thing they did was make him get up and walk. He assumed it was the same in this instance to ensure he wouldn't stiffen. Stiffness was also a symptom of tetanus, and he had to make sure he wasn't showing any signs of it.

"How far would you say we are from Harper Springs?" Steve asked as he cut one of the fish from tail to head.

Ryan looked around, trying to get a good vantage point. The bend in the river and the bridge helped him figure out how far down the highway they had gotten. "Rattlesnake Bridge is about three miles out from town. Back when things were normal, you'd hit houses and businesses before that. I even think there was a ranch house just over there, across the river." He pointed to the west, but there was nothing there. It was like life never even existed where Ryan had grown up.

"You think you can do three miles on that leg tomorrow?"

"I'm going to have to. Ty is in bad shape and so am I. I'm hoping we run into someone in town, but I'm thinking it's going to be the same story. Ghost towns with leveled houses and businesses with nothing to show for it except the foundations and torn up trees. But I can at least go to where my business was and see if there's anything I can gather. With a car, we could hightail it out of here and get out of the storm zone. I could find a hospital for Ty and me."

"And your wife?" Steve asked, glancing up from the fish.

Ryan took another sip from the canteen and screwed the lid back on. The question was a simple one, but complex in his mind. "She's dead, Steve." He choked on his words, his voice cracking. He had to look away to prevent Steve from seeing the tears gather in the corners of his eyes.

"How do you know that?"

"Look around us." He spread his hands wide. "Houses are gone. Horses and cattle are gone. Human existence, *almost* gone. The chances of her surviving all of this are slim to none."

"We did."

"I was lucky enough to be right by my cellar when it hit. My wife was in her car on the way to town."

"You can't say she's dead until you have proof. Don't give up, Ryan. The fact that we're still alive proves that this weather system didn't clean out every living thing. The coyotes made it. They are trouble for us, but there's more proof. And your son and dad. What about them? Didn't your dad travel from his ranch to get to you? He's still alive."

Ryan ducked his head and closed his eyes. Thinking that Cecilia was dead felt like a huge person was sitting on his shoulders. "Excuse me if I'm not Mr. Optimistic right now, Steve. Something tells me she's gone. Where's her car? She was right along this highway we've been following this whole time."

"I don't know what to tell you, Ryan. You gotta do what you gotta do. You've made it this far. No sense in stalling out now."

"I know. Just give me a minute. Once we start making

progress again, I'll feel better." He wasn't one for sitting still. Even though he was injured, the time they sat around to allow him to rest was time wasted. They were only three miles away from Harper Springs. Shouldn't they be running into more people? *Three miles!* That wasn't far, but it was like the fates were trying to keep him away for a reason.

DARRYL HAD LOST track of what day it was. His watch's battery had died, but he had somewhat of an idea of what time it was. When the sun would finally show through the clouds, he could estimate, but with the dusty haze and the dark skies, he spent most of his time trying to guess.

It didn't help that Ty kept asking him questions he didn't have answers to. There would come a time when he would have to decide to get Ty out of there and try to find someone who could help them. The food was running low, and though they had things to eat, they were both losing weight. They were rationing what they had, only able to eat small amounts that didn't provide near the caloric intake they needed to sustain their needs. With Ty injured, he needed more nutrients, but his appetite was gone, and Darryl had to force him to eat the little ration he could have.

His clothing was getting baggy. He tied some willow switches together to make a belt, but it barely held his pants up enough for him to get any work done. He needed energy, and the potted meat, crackers, and canned goods weren't good enough anymore.

He had stopped trying to gather supplies from the pasture. He used to take Ty with him to get him some fresh air, but the boy was so tired he didn't want to get up from the lawn chair. Darryl couldn't blame him – he didn't want to do much either. The lack of sun also put a damper on their moods. Things were going from bad to worse, and it was a bitter pill to swallow when he thought they were just slowly dying as they waited.

Doug was still tied up, and Darryl checked on him occasionally. The wound on his shin wasn't near as bad as Ty's arm, just a small scrape from the bullet graze. He hadn't said much but continuously glared at Darryl when they made eye contact. He'd eventually have to let the thief go. He was taking some of their food and it was another worry of Darryl's. Right now, freeing him wasn't an option. He was still angry, and Darryl couldn't risk retaliation against Ty or Ryan if Doug did eventually find him. For the most part, Doug was keeping to himself. It also could have been a game he was playing to manipulate Darryl. He couldn't let his guard down and had to be ready for anything.

He spent most of the day underground with Ty. With no motivation, there was no reason in wasting more energy.

"Ty?" Darryl always made a point to talk to him and make sure he was responsive. The child opened his eyes and looked at him but didn't say anything. "You hungry?"

"No."

"Thirsty?"

"No."

The fact that his grandson wasn't as talkative as before was also worrisome. He handed Ty a bottle of water. "Take a sip. I know you're not thirsty, but just take a sip."

Ty complied and handed it back to Darryl. "I feel really sick."

Darryl ran his hand over Ty's forehead. It was hot, his skin clammy and pale. He tried to hide his concern, but he had a fever, and it wasn't low-grade.

"Let me see your arm."

Ty didn't put up a fight, and Darryl gently unwrapped the injured area. The punctured skin from the protruding bone was red around the edges but didn't look too infected. He grabbed the first aid kit and sanitized his hands before slipping rubber gloves on. Dousing a cotton ball in alcohol, he lightly pressed it against Ty's skin.

"Does that hurt?"

CHAPTER TWENTY

Ryan nodded and closed his eyes. "Yes. Please don't do that. Please stop!"

Darryl did as Ty had asked. For days, Ty claimed he couldn't feel his arm. He finally learned what numb meant, and that's how he described how it felt. And today, it was a different story. Tears fell down his cheeks and against the dark circles under his eyes. He was as pale as a sheet, his lips dry and cracked from not getting enough water.

Shaking out two ibuprofen, Ty knew exactly what to do. He was becoming a pro at taking pills, and it left an unsettling feeling in the pit of Darryl's stomach. Over-the-counter pain medications were designed for short-term care for discomfort. Anything taken more often than advised meant liver damage. What was he supposed to do? Let the kid lay there in pain? The ibuprofen would also help get the fever down, but if his arm was infected, it wouldn't go away until they treated the underlying problem, which probably meant amputation. And Darryl certainly wasn't comfortable doing that on his own. He'd end up killing his grandson.

"I'm going up for a minute, Ty. I'll be right back."

Ty didn't open his eyes, but he nodded. Darryl had to make a decision. Ryan was probably dead. There was no way a man could survive on his own out there with the type of weather they had gotten. Darryl making it to his son's ranch was a fluke and he had gotten lucky. He hoped the story was the same with Ryan. Harper Springs was only about ten miles but walking it on a normal day was treacherous. In these conditions, it was damn near impossible.

If he hauled Ty toward town, death was inevitable. If they continued to wait around for help that wasn't coming, death was inevitable. Darryl sat down and contemplated his options, weighing the pros and cons of either decision.

If they stayed at the cellar, they had constant shelter for when the weather changed. They still had some food supply, but it was running out, and their rations were getting smaller each day. He could hunt, but his ammunition was low. The river wasn't too far, but that would mean leaving Ty unattended. He was so exhausted, he'd probably never realize Darryl had left him. If it came down to it, he'd go fish at the river. Staying there was a slow, miserable death. Darryl couldn't keep him alive forever.

If they left to find help, it meant no shelter, even more limited food, and they'd be exposed to looters, wild animals, and lord knew what else. But it also meant they were trying. And if the weather turned bad, the only saving grace would mean that they'd die fast, and all suffering would be over.

But what if Ryan was closing in on help for them? His son had always been stubborn and resourceful. If there was anyone he could trust to do what he promised, it was Ryan. And he'd do anything for his family. His going off to get help proved the type of man he was. It'd be horrible if he decided to take Ty and get help, and they narrowly missed Ryan on his way back.

If only he had a way of getting hold of him. He glanced over at Doug who had his head leaned back against the tree. If another storm threatened, he couldn't leave him there. That would be cruel, and even though Doug would probably leave him to die like that, Darryl didn't have it in him.

"You got something to say to me?" Doug asked. "You look like someone just ran over your dog."

"You sure are bold for a man who is tied up to a tree with a storm coming." Darryl pointed west toward the dark, swirling clouds.

"I'd prefer you leave me here. Why are you so set on surviving? We're all going to die eventually. Might as well make it quick."

"We've had a shift in attitude, haven't we?" Darryl smiled and handed him an apple. "Found it on a tree down the road. I forgot Ryan had a few apple trees on his place. There weren't many apples left, but I harvested a few. Not quite ripe, but a change from all the processed crap we've been eating."

"Why are you being nice to me?" Doug asked as he bit into

it. Juices flowed around his mouth. It must have been a better one than Darryl had just eaten.

"Being nice and being tolerant are two different things, Doug. I believe that if people come together in times like this, we can get a lot of stuff done." He adjusted the bandana around his neck and looked at the sky. "Guys like you take advantage of situations like this, and look where it landed you."

"And you're better off? That kid over there is worse off than me, and you shot me! All you two are doing is dying slow, old man. Take that gun of yours, put three bullets in the chamber, do us all a favor, and kill us now! It'll be quick and painless."

"And us giving up," Darryl replied.

"No, us accepting reality! What good is staying alive when we're in a wasteland? Your son is dead! Don't you think he'd be back by now if he wasn't?"

Darryl ran his hand through his hair and took a deep breath. It was like Doug could read his mind. "I can't believe that Doug. I don't think he's dead. I think he's going to come back."

"Your mouth says one thing, but your face says otherwise. You think he's dead, but if you keep saying he's not, it'll make you feel better."

"I know my son. You don't."

"Do your grandson a favor, Darryl. Kill us and then off yourself. Put us out of our damn misery!"

Doug yelled and his voice traveled for miles. Darryl didn't know what to say, so he walked away, torn between staying or going. A storm was on its way, which bought him some time to mull it over. After it passed through, he'd make up his mind and stick with whatever plan he came up with.

CHAPTER TWENTY-ONE

Getting through the night was rough. Between the constant pain in Ryan's leg and the howling coyotes, sleep was impossible. He had never held onto his gun tighter, and any time he sensed something coming up on him and Steve, he sat up, ready to shoot whatever it was. Two encounters with coyotes were enough, and it likely wasn't over just yet. With evidence of rabies, it meant that other animals were likely infected, which meant fear of coming up to humans was gone, replaced by a desire to attack anything that got in their way.

The sun began to come up on the horizon, and Ryan moved his leg to gauge how painful it was going to be to stand up. There was a deep ache in his thigh, but it wasn't as bad as the initial injury. He double-checked the bandage and put his hands on the ground, pushing his body weight upward. He groaned out in pain but tried to keep quiet. Steve was sleeping next to the smoldering embers left from the night before, and he didn't want him to see his struggle.

Using the tree for support, Ryan got to a standing position and kept all his weight on his good leg. Gritting his teeth, he took a step, limping as he went along. He couldn't walk as fast as normal, but the fact that he was moving again made him feel almost human. Blood flowed through him, and though he hadn't gotten any sleep, he hit his second wind.

The injured leg did hurt, and the tension of the homemade stitches burned. He had to take it easy so he wouldn't rip them. After a couple of laps around their campsite, he zipped up his jeans and fastened his belt. He had lost some weight during their trek toward town, so the denim was loose around the wound, helping keep the dirty fabric from infecting him.

"It's good to see you up and moving. How do you feel?" Steve lifted his head and stretched out.

"Like a million bucks."

"You're a damn liar," Steve replied, laughing. "What, no coffee? What the hell are you good for?"

"Get your ass up. If a storm comes, I can't run. It's still cool out, which means no daytime heating. We're not far and we can make it to Harper Springs in an hour if we start now. If things go as planned."

They gathered up their supplies and made sure the fire was out. Ryan handed him a packet of crackers and they shared. His limp was very pronounced, and he found a decent-sized walking stick to help with his balance. They crossed the river again and filled up their canteens.

"Last time we'll cross it. But it won't be much longer now."

"You think there will actually be people in town?"

"Yes. If I think anything different, there's no point in going."

Neither spoke for a while as they walked. Ryan got lost in all the what if's they could run into. It was hard to keep control of taking things as they came. They had crossed so many bridges, made decisions at crossroads, and there were still so many possibilities of how things would play out. Ty and Cecilia – his two main inspirations – his driving force to keep going even though he had a gaping hole patched up by sewing thread.

"Ryan, did you notice the sky?" Steve asked. "We better hope that's just rain."

"Son of a..." Ryan looked back, his heart skipping a beat.

"That's more than rain." There was a large hail shaft almost a mile wide, close enough that he could hear the hailstones pelting the ground. The temperature fell, and the cold air was another indication hail was imminent.

The constant pain in Ryan's leg was a huge reminder that he couldn't run like he used to. But with the storm still south and making that much noise, it was going to be a big system. Every storm since this all began averaged baseball to softball-sized, with bigger slabs of ice falling in between. His hypothesis of this one being damaging wasn't hard to believe.

They were very close to Harper Springs. He could see the population sign, dangling off a metal pole, swaying in the wind. But the population sign still meant they had another mile before they even reached the center part of the town where his shop and all the shelters were. It'd be a long run to beat the storm, and it still wasn't a guarantee they'd find somewhere to hide.

He'd take his chances. The wind picked up, and thunder rumbled. "C'mon, Steve, we gotta get moving."

"But your leg!"

"To hell with my leg or we're dead men! If we don't outrun this, my leg won't even matter."

He felt the stitches rip as he ran. The pain was almost unbearable, but with a massive storm right behind him, it was enough inspiration to push through the pain and get to safety. Warm blood soaked into his jeans and trickled downward. It'd be an ugly mess when all was said and done, or maybe it wouldn't matter. If they couldn't get somewhere safe, he'd be dead anyway.

Hail came out of the sky like huge bombs. Steve was right in front of him, splashing through large puddles, the mud serving as quicksand, hindering them from going faster. Ryan's lungs burned. His leg ached. He couldn't count how many times he got pelted with hail. But he kept moving. He was going to win this battle. He came too far to let it all end right there, with Harper Springs just over the hill.

The wind was so strong that it sucked them backward like a

CHAPTER TWENTY-ONE

vacuum. Steve held onto Ryan, and they hopped into a ravine that was about five feet deep. It had some water in the bottom, but if they crouched down, the dirt walls would serve as a small barrier, separating them from the hail stones and flying debris.

Ryan watched the sky overhead. Cloud-to-cloud lightning flashed, and the dark clouds were ominously beautiful. The storm was right over them, horizontal rain, wind, and loud crackles of thunder pushing through, ready to devour whoever stood in its way. Ryan gripped the dirt around him, needing something to hold onto out of instinct. He hadn't spotted any more hail, and the storm dissipated, leaving behind rain and light wind. The trees danced in the breeze and the water in the ravine was deeper. If the storm had moved slower, the possibility of drowning would've been a horrible reality. But somehow, they had escaped another temper tantrum from Mother Nature.

"We gotta get you some help, Ryan." Steve pointed to his leg. "It's bleeding again."

"But I'm breathing," Ryan replied. "You get hit?"

Steve touched his forehead and looked at the blood on his fingertips. "Didn't even feel it. I'll be damned."

They climbed out of the ravine and Ryan limped toward the highway. The sun was out like nothing had happened. "Damn you, Mother Nature."

"Is that Harper Springs?"

Ryan shielded his eyes from the sun, the sight in front of him haunting. It was Harper Springs, but not the small town he had remembered. Though he was expecting the town to be leveled, his breath caught in his throat when he took a moment to scan the horizon and observe the destruction in front of him. Knowing it happened was one thing... seeing it put it all into perspective.

Foundations were the only piece of evidence that proved a building ever stood there. Groves of trees were stripped of their leaves and small branches, leaving stumps. Small piles of rubble and debris were scattered across the area, which gave him a small shred of hope that there were people around, attempting to get things cleaned up.

"Where is everyone?" he asked, taking a step closer. Vehicles were turned over and none appeared to be in working order. "Keep an eye out for a car that might work for us. It'd be quicker than trying to fix Mrs. McElroy's."

"Holy shit, it's like a bomb hit!" Steve surveyed the area, running from debris pile to debris pile. "I wonder who is here."

Ryan didn't know what to say. The town he knew and loved was leveled. Childhood memories at the park were gone. Houses destroyed. Businesses tore up - people's way of life, their income and hard work... wiped off the face of the earth. Would they ever be able to bounce back from this? Did they even want to?

"Ryan! Ryan Gibson!" He heard the voice in the distance.

Ryan hobbled on his strong leg. Squinting into the sun, he saw a person about half a mile down the road, waving at him. He still couldn't make out who it was, but signs of another human life lit a fire under Ryan, his pessimism replaced by a small twinge of hope.

"Ryan!" The person yelled again, his arms waving.

Was it Chief Rayburn? Ryan walked as fast as he could. They finally met in the middle of the road. The Chief looked in almost as bad of shape as he was in. He had lost a lot of weight and his arms were covered in cuts and wounds.

"Chief Rayburn! What in the hell is going on?"

"No one knows for sure, but it's not just us. This destruction is at least statewide and likely across the country. We have no way of calling out or getting information, which is why the assumption is this is much larger than a regional issue. It's like Revelations is really happening."

"You're not the first person to say that to me."

"How many people have you come across out there?"

"Not too many. I picked up this guy. He's been a good help to me. Steve, this is Chief Rayburn."

CHAPTER TWENTY-ONE

They shook hands and Chief Rayburn's eyes fell on Ryan's leg. "We need to get you some medical attention!"

"I don't have time. I'm trying to find Cecilia. And I gotta get back to Ty. He's hurt worse than me, and I don't even know..." he tried to keep his voice from shaking. "I don't even know if he's still alive. It's been a couple of weeks since I left to get help and..."

"Who is with him?"

"My father. Who is here in town? Who made it?"

Chief Rayburn patted Ryan on the shoulder, his eyes downcast. "Not many. But we have a temporary emergency room going on over at the Baptist church in the basement. And the basement at the Methodist church is being used as a... as a morgue, Ryan."

"A morgue?"

"We go out and try and find people who need help, but you've seen the weather. If we go too far, we're all dead. We've found a few alive, but we're finding twice that many who are dead. We'll have to find another place to put the bodies soon."

"Have you found Cecilia, Chief? Be straight with me."

"Let's head over to the churches, Ryan. You need to get that leg fixed up, and your friend Steve here needs his head looked at. You can't help Ty if you can't even walk."

The fact that Chief Rayburn didn't want to answer him made Ryan fear he'd find Cecilia at the Methodist church in the morgue. Maybe he hadn't seen her. The walk to the churches was sad. He could point out where people's houses were, where he and Cecilia loved to go eat, and the park where Ty always asked to go play at when they were running errands. And now it was a war zone.

A nurse Ryan didn't recognize triaged him and made him sit on a gurney. There weren't very many people around, so she was able to get to him quickly. He imagined it was a different scene across the street, with lifeless bodies strewn across the cement floor.

"If Cecilia is at the Methodist Church, just say it, Chief. I need to know. I don't have time to..."

"Ryan?"

There was no mistaking the voice, and when he looked her way, he felt the warmth fall down his cheeks. Cecilia was standing by the basement door, her midsection wrapped in an ace bandage. She also looked thinner and exhausted, but Ryan had never seen her so beautiful. Ignoring the nurse's warning to stay still, he scooped his wife up into his arms and kissed her, overcome with joy, forgetting about the chaos around him.

"Where's Ty?" Cecilia pulled away.

"Back at home in the cellar. My dad is with him. Listen, Cecilia, he's hurt. He's hurt bad."

"What happened?" Her eyes were wide, tears gathering in the corners.

"His arm and his head. Happened right when the first storm hit. I guess during the commotion of getting him down in the shelter it happened, but I wouldn't even be able to tell you how. He's alive. And I left them with food. I came looking for you and I'm so glad you're safe. But now I need to get back to Ty and bring him here. Now he has real help who can get him out of that cellar and give him some medical attention.

Cecilia nodded and a stray tear fell down her face. Ryan swiped it away with his index finger. "It's so dangerous out there, Ryan." She whispered, ducking her head. "But I know if there is anyone who can get our baby here, it's you."

"I'll do anything I can to make sure it happens."

"I'm so scared, Ryan. Everyone is talking about the end of the world. Tornadoes, landslides, earthquakes, typhoons. Everyone on the planet is supposedly going through some kind of weather phenomenon."

"I guess we won't know the truth until we can make contact with people out there."

"I thought I'd never see you again. I thought you and Ty had died. I got so lucky. I stopped by Chief Rayburn's house on the way in that day. His wife wanted to give me some zucchini from her garden. And as soon as I got out of the car, they were pulling me into safety. And then, we ended up here. It's all a blur. I can't even remember most of the details. But I've spent most of my time worrying about you and my baby."

"And your parents? Have you heard from them?"

Cecilia shook her head and more tears fell. "No. The rescue teams are trying to get out there, but you know how it is. You came all the way from the house to here. That's nothing short of a miracle."

"And I've gotta go back. I've got to get Ty and Dad. I found Mrs. McElroy's car. It's flooded, but if I can get enough tools, I can rig it up enough to drive and turn a long trip on foot into a quick one behind the wheel. Finding the tools will be the hard part." He held her hand, probably squeezing too tight. "What's with the Ace bandage?"

"Cracked rib. It's not helping, but there's not much the medical staff can do. They were able to scrounge up a few things and it's better than nothing."

"Look at us. It's like we've gotten hit by a damn freight train."

That made Cecilia smile, and she tiptoed and pecked Ryan on the lips. "I guess technically we have. Isn't that the way all of us southern people describe the way twisters sound on the news? Like a big train?"

Ryan laughed and kissed the top of her head. "Everything is going to be fine. I promise."

"Mr. Gibson, we need to look at your leg." The nurse motioned him toward the gurney. "Sit right here and relax. We'll have you feeling better in no time."

Ryan couldn't tell if she meant it or was being sarcastic. With the lack of medical equipment available, he was sure it was the latter.

CHAPTER TWENTY-TWO

After an IV of fluids and a thorough cleaning of his wound, Ryan felt like a new man. The nurse had done a good job of stitching him back up, and with a clean pair of pants, the chances of infection had been reduced. Cecilia had put it correctly – everything had been a blur.

Harper Springs was a small town, but the lack of people around was shocking. There were maybe ten people in the respite area. He didn't have the stomach to go across the street to the morgue. He'd probably recognize more people there, and he couldn't handle seeing folks he knew, laid out like trash. Out of sight, out of mind, and if he hadn't officially seen their lifeless bodies, it gave him hope that most of his friends were still alive, just holding out until someone came to rescue them.

Going against medical advice, he went back up to ground level to begin his search for tools to fix the car, or another means of transportation to get back to his cellar. There were several trashed cars around town, but most were in even worse shape than being flooded.

Steve got his head stitched up and was helping him. When he got to the area of town where his shop was located, he wasn't surprised to see leveled buildings and no one around. The two cars he had left in the garage were gone. One was an old Ford Bronco and the other was a Chevy Camaro. He stopped in front of where Mrs. McElroy's bakery once stood and took his baseball cap off, taking a moment of silence for her.

He found a couple of wrenches pushed down in the dirt, and a few car parts that wouldn't be compatible with the Dodge Neon. Sifting through debris piles, he came up short, but he was able to gather a couple of towels and a hammer to add to his arsenal. He was going to have to get creative when fixing the car and doubted his capabilities with his limited resources.

Nightfall set in over the area, and the moon was bright, the stars twinkling, giving false security to the ones left behind.

"Let's call it a night and get back to the church," Ryan said. "And Steve, you don't have to help me. Stay here where it's safe. I appreciate all that you've done, but this isn't your problem."

"What else have I got to do?"

Ryan knew good help was hard to find, and though he still didn't know much about Steve, he was thankful for the bond they had developed. He found Cecilia in the far corner of the basement. Thankfully it was a big enough area, and with not many around, they had some privacy. What he'd give to have a moment alone with her, but neither was in good enough shape to even think about it.

"Find anything you can use?" Cecilia asked, pulling the blankets back on the pallet she had made.

"Not really. And even if I did, it's still a good hike back to where we left the car. I don't know what the hell I'm gonna do, Cecilia."

"You'll figure it out, Ryan. And I was thinking. I want to come with you."

Ryan shook his head and bit his bottom lip. "Say that again. I want to make sure I heard you right."

"I want to come with you. He's my son too. I want to help him."

"No, that's not a good idea."

"Why not?"

"What if something happens to us? You wanna leave Ryan without both parents?"

"You can't talk like that." She pulled her knees up to her chest and rested her head on them. "All this time apart and all I could think was that you were dead. Now you're here and I don't want to let you out of my sight. But we have to get our baby, Ryan. And the only way to keep you near to me is to go. I want to help Ty just as badly as you do."

Ryan was too tired to argue with her, but he couldn't let it go. "Both of us getting killed out there isn't going to help him. I can get back to him. I made it this far. I can do it again."

Cecilia opened her mouth to say something but stopped herself and looked away. Ryan guided her to face him again, his index finger under her chin. Leaning in, he skimmed his lips over hers, gently kissing her, his free hand sliding down the side of her breast.

She pulled away first, smoothing her hands down her hair. "You're going to come back safe to me, right?" It was a whisper, and so quiet that Ryan had to read her lips.

"I am. And Ty will too. And then we'll work on finding your parents. You're a damn good woman for wanting to come, but for me, please stay here. Will you do that for me?"

She nodded and closed her eyes, kissing him again. "I love you, Ryan. I still can't believe this is happening."

"Me either. Let's get some rest. Tomorrow is a new day. One step at a time, yeah?"

Cecilia smirked and laid back on the blankets. "I guess there's one plus to all of this."

"What's that?"

"Your attitude. The Ryan from before wasn't too good at the one step at a time plan."

If only she knew the inner struggle he had faced every day. Some things were best left unsaid.

Snuggling beside her, he hugged her from behind. Burying his face in her neck, he almost felt guilty for relaxing with Ty was still out there in danger. But he couldn't pull himself away. It felt like he'd wake up and it'd all be a dream, and he'd have to accept the reality that Cecilia was gone. The scent of her hair and the feel of her skin against him confirmed this was happening, even if it seemed too good to be true.

AFTER THE STORM PASSED, Darryl stuck true to his word. Ty was suffering, they were hungry, and he couldn't sit around and wait, watching his grandson die a slow, painful death. Water was low, food was even lower, and now that he had a fever, the sense of urgency was intensified.

He found a duffel bag in the cabinet and filled it with water and the rest of the food. Ty was asleep, and Darryl didn't know if the boy would even be able to walk, much less trek the twelve miles into Harper Springs.

"Ty?" Darryl gently touched his shoulder, but he was a sound sleeper, so he nudged him again, a little harder the second time. "Ty?"

His eyelids fluttered open, and he blinked a few times, squinting against the lantern beside the lawn chair. "Grandpa?"

"You ready to go?"

"Where are we going?"

His eyes lit up some, but with the dark circles and bags around them, he didn't look like the same kid Darryl once knew. "I'm going to take you and get some help. Sound good?"

Ty nodded and sat up, and Darryl skimmed his hand across his forehead. His skin was still blazing hot and sweaty, and his eyes looked heavy. He was running a higher fever than the last time he checked him, and he couldn't bring himself to shove another painkiller down his throat.

"Can you walk?" Darryl asked.

"Yeah, I can walk."

"I'm going to carry you up."

They got to ground level and Darryl remembered Doug, tied up, suddenly a hitch in his plan. What in the hell was he going to do with him? Ty followed him to the stranger, but Darryl kept himself between the two of them in case Doug tried to do something in retaliation. It never occurred to him to take Doug in when the storm hit, but it turned out to be nothing more than rain anyway, the stronger weather staying north of them. His mind had been on Ty, and he was thankful the weather wasn't severe. Even with Doug's history, he wouldn't be able to live with himself if he suffered.

"What are your plans, Doug?"

Doug looked up at Darryl in surprise, his eyes wide as if the question was taboo. "I already told you what I want you to do. A free pass to kill me and you won't do it. You sure didn't hesitate when you shot me."

"It's a scratch. You're fine. And I'm not going to kill you. I don't think you really want me to do it."

"Are you leaving?"

"We are." Darryl didn't want to go into more detail with him. He still didn't trust the man, which was why it was so damn hard letting him go.

"That's a death sentence. You two won't last the day out there."

"I'm willing to take my chances. No one is coming. It's a death sentence if we stay here. And I don't have to justify a damn thing to you, Doug. You're the one who decided to loot. You're the one who tried to take advantage of others, which got your brother killed. I don't blame Ryan for locking you in that cellar."

Doug looked away, the mention of his brother silencing him. "That's a blow below the belt, old man. You asked what my plans were?"

"Yeah." Darryl shook his head. For a second, he felt some sympathy for Doug.

"Just leave me here. Tied to this tree."

"You don't want me to do that. I know you don't."

Doug clenched his jaw and looked up at Darryl. "If you let me go, I'm going to come after you. I'm going to go find Ryan and finish the job, for my brother. I can't let him die in vain. So, your best bet, old man, is to just keep me where I am."

"If you're so dead set on taking out revenge on my family, why tell me? Why not let me untie you and then do it?"

Doug didn't answer him and dug his heel into the soft ground.

"I know why. Suicide by way of reverse psychology." Darryl laughed and swiped the sweat from the back of his neck. The humidity felt like it was picking up again, which meant they needed to get moving or be stuck there even longer. "I'm not going to let you do that. I'm not going to help you kill yourself."

Kneeling, he untied the ropes, and when he stood up, he kept one hand on the butt of the gun in his pocket just in case Doug had a change of heart. He could have been playing him all along, trying for the sympathy card, and Darryl couldn't risk it. But Doug didn't do anything. He got to his feet, dusted his pants off, and checked the bandage over his shin. The wound wasn't bad at all, and he'd be fine to walk.

"Just keep in mind, I have the gun. I'm going to watch your every move. You're coming with us to Harper Springs."

"Can't you just let a man be? Why take me along?"

"For several reasons, Doug. I see potential in you. If you can lead a string of looting and mayhem, you can lead for something good. And I also can't keep looking over my shoulder if we do go our separate ways. I don't know you. I can't risk you coming back and finishing the job, as you put it."

Doug hoisted his backpack on his shoulder and scoffed. "Going north is our funeral, but since I want you to put me out of my misery anyway, you have no objection from me. We'll be dead long before Harper Springs is on the horizon."

Ryan woke up early the next morning. The rescue team had brought in another victim, and it was a teenage boy who wasn't in good shape. He had blood stained down his face from what looked like a head injury, and just like everyone else, he looked tired, hungry, and ready for all of it to be over. He seemed familiar, but Ryan couldn't place his name. He knew him from somewhere.

Cecilia stirred beside him, and he smiled, gently kissing her cheek as she sat up and stretched.

"Best night of sleep I've gotten since the night before hell on earth started," Ryan said, kissing her again. "Hey, who is that kid they just brought in? How do I know him?"

Cecilia yawned and looked in that direction. "Hard to tell with all that blood on his face." They both watched in silence for a few minutes, and she snapped her fingers and said, "That's Bryson Taylor! Basketball star of the Harper Springs Panthers. Starting point guard two years in a row and he's just a junior."

"That's right! Damn, talk about a reality check. At least they found someone else alive. We're outnumbered in comparison to the church across the street."

"And you better not add to it, Ryan. I thought about it a lot last night. Is this our way of life now? Staying underground, small portions of food, and someone has to risk their lives to get to the river for water? There's no quality of life in that scenario."

"No, there's not," Ryan agreed, holding her hand. "Something has to give. This can't be a new normal. I have to believe that."

"Me too. And you're a good man for everything you've done. Just make sure you come back to me. Make sure I see sweet little Ty again."

"You know I will." He pulled her in for a hug, kissing the top

CHAPTER TWENTY-TWO

of her head. "I am gonna go back out there and see what else I can find. I'll check in with you in an hour."

When he stood up, his leg felt even sorer than the day before. The tension of the stitches made his stomach clench, remembering the pain ripping through his body when he had to outrun the storm. He'd probably have the limp for a long time and hopefully, it wouldn't be something permanent.

Steve joined him outside. They went back to the former area of Ryan's shop and dug through debris piles. It was hard staying positive, but Ryan made himself not fall into a negative slump. The fact that he had found Cecilia alive was a boost to get him out of the rut he found himself in just a few days ago.

"Are you the one who is looking for a vehicle?"

Ryan looked up and saw Tommy Wilson coming up the road. He was a fellow firefighter in the department with him, and it was great to see a familiar face.

"Tommy! Good to see you!" Ryan shook his hand and spread his arms. "Just going through all this shit. Hoping to find something salvageable from my shop. Coming up empty-handed."

"I've heard some crazy tornado stories about them blowing away one house and leaving the one next door untouched. And that urban legend about the bible in the church being turned to Revelations. But this is all new to me. It's like Harper Springs never existed. The cement slab below us is the only hint."

Ryan motioned toward Steve and introduced the two men. "This is Steve. He's new to the area. He's helped me out a lot getting here."

"Oh yeah, I know you. We met about a month ago. You were looking into buying some goats from me."

"That's right! I don't reckon you have any left," Steve said, laughing.

"Couldn't answer that. Some animals are making their way back. Some are still missing. I figure most didn't survive. I'm helping on the rescue team. Every day, I swear the ratio is five to one on the dead people we bring in."

"As soon as I get my son here, I'll help with that, but I'm sort of a one-man rescue squad myself, with the help of Steve here."

"Your son is missing?" A genuine look of concern flashed across Tommy's face.

"No. He's back at my place with my dad. He got hurt during that first round that came through. I came to town to get help and find Cecilia. Now I need to get back to him. We came across a car down by the river, but it's flooded, so I'm trying to find anything I can to patch it up and get it running long enough to make it out there. It's too far to bring him on foot."

"No, don't do that." Tommy shook his head. "We've got a couple of horses over at the church. They were part of the livestock I was talking about that randomly showed back up. You know, they say to watch a horse when the weather is getting bad. They have the best instincts about what is coming. They also have great instincts in finding their way back home."

"How many horses do you have?"

"Three so far. Take one! You'll have better luck than wasting more time trying to fix a car. I know you're a damn fine mechanic but get that boy back here. Get him back with his mama."

"I wouldn't be imposing on the rescue team?"

"Hell no! We're taking a break anyhow. Don't make me tell you again. Take one!"

Ryan didn't have to be told twice. It wouldn't be as fast as a car, but it would be better than walking. And with about a day's hike back to Mrs. McElroy's car, taking a horse was the break he was needing.

Chief Rayburn saddled up a paint horse and said, "She's the fastest one we have. If we don't see you by tomorrow evening, we'll head that way. Be careful, Ryan. I don't have to tell you how dangerous it is out there."

"Yes, sir. And thank you for letting me do this."

"Get going. Can't wait to see that boy of yours."

Ryan hopped on the horse and pulled on the reins, pointing

her south of town. His thigh burned, but it was the last thing on his mind. Lightning flashed in the distance. Tommy was right – a horse had great instincts when it came to weather. He'd keep one eye on the sky and one eye on her behavior. Help was coming for Ty if he could just hold on a little longer. His family would be together again soon.

CHAPTER TWENTY-THREE

Ryan gripped the reins tight as he galloped away from Harper Springs. It was hard leaving Cecilia there. She wanted to go, and he wanted to stay, but he had to save Ty. With as long as he had been away from him, he feared the worst – what if they ran out of food and water? What if a looter got them? A lot could happen during their time apart.

"You didn't have to come with me." Ryan looked over at Steve, who was becoming a good pal that he appreciated. Without his company and help, finding Cecilia and getting that far never would have been possible.

"What else would I be doing? Sitting around the storm shelter, twiddling my thumbs? Forget about it, Ryan. And when we make it back with all your family accounted for, I'll help the rescue team go out and get others. No sense in wasting time."

"You're a good man, Steve. Going out of your way for people you don't even know. That's a trait not too many people have anymore."

"I may not be here from here, but I come from a place that has similar values to Harper Springs. Everyone here is family now. I'll do what I can to help."

Ryan nodded and watched the sun move behind some thick

clouds on the horizon. Keeping Tommy's advice in mind, he kept an eye on his horse, looking out for any erratic behavior that would tip him off to changing weather. Right now, the clouds weren't too ominous to worry about, but with as fast as things had changed, he couldn't let his guard down.

There was also a slight dip in temperature, which was a refreshing change. Instead of going back and forth between the river and the highway, Ryan took a more direct route to his house. It would cut off a few miles, but it meant riding through more un-level ground and wooded areas. Steve seemed to be handling the horse well, and he was glad he knew how to ride. He was certain they'd have to run them at full speed at some point during their trip.

"You up for a change in snacks?" Ryan pointed ahead of them, his mouth watering at the thought.

"Is that a vineyard?"

"Damn right, it is. Now, if we can find some grapes that aren't all smashed up and ruined from the storm, that will be a miracle." Ryan sped up the horse and jumped off at the edge of a rows of grapes.

As predicted, most had been torn up from the weather. Old, rotted grapes were on the ground at their feet, and Ryan lifted the leaves and plants to see if there was anything to scrounge up. He'd love to gather up just enough for Ty – the boy could eat a whole bag of grapes by himself.

"I forgot this is a big grape area," Steve said, plucking a withered one from the stem.

"Yeah. These aren't really to eat. They're more for wine. But hell, I'll take it if I can find any that aren't ruined."

As they moved in closer to the middle of the vineyard, Ryan found a cluster worth gathering, and he ate a few, savoring the juice as it trickled down his chin. It was a nice sugar boost, giving him the energy he wasn't expecting.

He put a few in a plastic bag and kept it separate from the rest of his stuff. The grapes were already fragile, and he didn't want to smash them. He ate a few more and saved the rest for Ty. It was something different to eat and a morale booster, and once he and Steve were satisfied, they mounted up and continued south toward his land.

With the clouds back building in the distance, he quickened their pace. On horseback, the ride shouldn't take long. With each step they took, it felt like his farm was getting farther away. The anticipation was killing him. He couldn't wait to get Ty back to town and receive some medical attention. He also couldn't wait for Cecilia to be reunited with her son. The look of fear and worry on her face was like a punch to the gut, and getting them all back together would be a relief for everyone.

"My place is right up there." Ryan nudged his boot into the side of the horse, and each time his hooves hit the ground below, it made his thigh sear with pain. He was half a mile from seeing his son again, and nothing was going to slow him down.

Steve was behind him, easily keeping up. Ryan slid off the horse and attempted to run to the cellar, but his body wouldn't allow it. Instead, he walked as fast as he could, swung open the homemade metal door he had concocted, and his heart sank when he saw that no one was inside.

"Dad? Ty?"

The wind blew around them, and distant thunder rumbled. He glanced at Steve, and then into the dark cellar. "Dad?"

"Maybe they went to town," Steve suggested, but Ryan ignored him.

"I hope that's the case. I hope someone didn't get them!" Ryan looked around the pasture. His dad had been busy tying together branches for rope, and he did a decent job of rebuilding steps for the cellar, but past that, there was no sign that they had been there.

Grabbing his flashlight from his bag, he turned it on and went down into the storm shelter. There was no food or supplies there. It was as if it had vanished.

Sighing, he looked up at Steve. "I guess that's a good sign. Maybe my dad took it all with them. But where did they go?" He thought about his question for a second. He tried hard not to jump to the worst-case scenario. "Maybe we should go back to the river. If I know my dad, he'll follow it to town so they're by the water."

"I think that's a good plan, Ryan. He probably got tired of waiting and decided to try and get some help on his own."

Ryan scoffed and shook his head. "That sounds like him. He's more impatient than me, and I never thought that would be possible."

DARRYL REGRETTED LEAVING THE CELLAR. With the clouds building behind them, he knew they had to hurry. They weren't too far from their safe haven, and if they backtracked, they could take cover before the weather hit. Ty was struggling, and now with Doug along for the ride, it felt like an anchor was weighing them down.

He stopped often, allowing time for Ty to rest, giving him water and snacks. He stayed by the river, so the worry of running out of water had faded. Their food supply was decent, but what Ty needed was protein, and if he could catch a fish, he'd build a fire and cook it. But with the impending weather that was likely headed their way, he didn't have time to stop and think, much less breathe.

"I told you we'd be dead before we reached town," Doug said, pointing behind them. "Unless some miracle comes along in the next hour, we're dead."

Darryl looked down at Ty, hating that his grandson could hear all the negativity. "Who says it'll come this way?"

"It's completely to the south of us. It's moving north. I'm no meteorologist, but it doesn't take a genius to figure it out."

"The storms have been unpredictable. You never know."

"If you don't want to die, old man, you should probably go back to your cellar and let me go."

Darryl shook his head and stopped, watching the swirling clouds, hoping they'd give him some indication of a shift southward. "I'm not letting you go, Doug. And we're not going to die." He nudged Ty and smiled, hoping to reassure the child. "Besides, I can't have you running around loose. I've already seen what you're capable of."

"Nah." Doug let out a sarcastic laugh. "I'm just going to stand out in an open field and let the twister suck me right up. Like I said earlier – put us all out of our damn misery!"

"The anchor on top of the thunderhead is pointing east. It's going to miss us to the south." Darryl was certain his observation was correct, but as unpredictable as everything had been, he didn't want to stick around and find out.

"How much farther, Grandpa?" Ty sighed as they walked.

"A little ways, but we're getting closer with each step."

"You gotta be shitting me," Doug replied, laughing again.

Darryl didn't bother to press the matter. Doug's snarky attitude was annoying, and if he didn't give him attention, maybe he'd be quiet. Silence was better than Ty being exposed to Doug's ignorance and negativity.

A small rain shower came through, which heightened Darryl's nerves. Something as simple as sprinkles could quickly grow within seconds, leaving them right in the middle of a death trap. He couldn't fail Ryan. He promised he'd take care of Ty. He also couldn't fail Ty. He still had his whole life to live, and hopefully, things would get back to normal once they reached other human beings. This could easily be an isolated event, or it could be spread farther than anyone could comprehend. It was a worry Darryl couldn't think about. Short term goals were the name of the game, and getting Ty some medical attention was the frontrunner on his to-do list.

"Call me crazy, but am I seeing someone on a horse?" Doug asked, shielding his eyes from the sun.

CHAPTER TWENTY-THREE

Darryl didn't take it seriously at first. Doug had cried wolf before, and he couldn't stomach falling for it again. But when he looked up, he did a double take. Was that Ryan? If it was, who was with him?

"Call *me* crazy, Doug, but I think this might be the miracle you were talking about just a few minutes ago."

RYAN COULDN'T BELIEVE he was playing 'hunt down the family member' again. He couldn't blame his dad for leaving – he had lost track of how long he had been gone, but he probably would have grown impatient as well. Time worked against them, and with each second that passed, hope trickled away with it.

He munched on a few more grapes, making sure to save enough for Ty. Hopefully, they'd still be good once he found them... *if* they found them. Staying positive was always hard for him, but even worse now. Finding Cecilia had helped, but now that his father and child were missing, he reverted right back to hating the world again.

"I see some people up near a grove of trees." Steve patted him on the shoulder, pulling him from his daydream. "Two men and a kid, it looks like."

Ryan squinted, guiding the horse with one hand as he tried to get a good look. "Two men? It should be just my dad and Ty. This might not be them." He approached with caution. He didn't want to step in the crossfire of another looter situation.

As they got closer, there was no doubt it was Ty and his father. He sprinted the horse until he approached them, his heart racing when he got a good look. Dismounting, he pulled Ty in for a hug, the same emotions flooding him that happened when he finally found Cecilia. He didn't even bother to look at the stranger who was with them.

Ryan smoothed the hair on Ty's forehead. The kid needed a haircut and a bath. He was paler than when he had left, and the light behind his eyes was gone. No wonder his dad decided to leave. Ty was suffering.

"I guess he's not going to acknowledge me."

Ryan looked over at the stranger, finally realizing who it was. "What the..." Jerking his head toward his dad, he pointed with his thumb. "Why in the hell is he here?"

"He came looking for you. I shot him in the shin. Now I'm taking him into town. That's the cliff notes version. His name is Doug, and I wasn't going to leave him behind."

Ryan darted his eyes back and forth between the two. "I suppose you have your reasons. Just like you have your reasons for taking Ty away from the cellar."

"As you can see, we need help. I couldn't wait any longer, Ryan. I guess you can do the same and introduce me to your friend."

"This is Steve. I met him when I ran across this guy." He pointed at the looter. "He's been helping me ever since."

"I have a name. It's Doug."

Ryan ignored him and cradled Ty in his arms. "We should probably get going. I don't like the look of the sky, and Cecilia is waiting back in Harper Springs. The longer I'm gone, the more worried she'll be. And Ty needs a doctor."

"You found her?" Darryl asked, scooting toward the horse. "I also see you got good transportation. This will cut down on travel time significantly."

"I found a broken-down car I was gonna fix, but this was quicker. A guy on the fire department with me offered us a couple horses, so I jumped on the opportunity. And I'm glad I did. I'm not sure how far y'all would've gotten before another storm came through."

Ryan hopped on the horse and placed Ty in front of him, his arms holding him on the saddle like two seatbelts. Darryl climbed in behind. "Doug can hop on with Steve."

"My arm hurts, Daddy. And I'm tired."

Ryan kissed the top of his head. "You ready to see Mommy?"

CHAPTER TWENTY-THREE

He pulled out the bag of grapes and Ty devoured them like they were candy.

"I am!" There was a small flash of energy inside the small child.

"Then let's get to town. You'll feel better soon."

They'd be together again soon and hopefully, they'd have a clearer picture of what had happened. It would be a time of rebuilding and getting back to normal. Or it could be continued chaos. Ryan had no idea what to expect.

If only they had seen it coming. If only they had been prepared. The difference in a couple of seconds could have changed the past month.

If only...

RYAN'S STORY CONTINUES WITH...

Ryan Gibson has finally been reunited with his wife and son in the makeshift refuge of the old church cellar. Harper Springs is still reeling from the devastating tornadoes that have ravaged the town, but the stormy skies have given way to scorching heat, signaling a dangerous shift in the climate. Fear and uncertainty grip the survivors as they contemplate the wrath of Mother Nature and the perilous challenges that lie ahead.

As they strive to rebuild their shattered community, Ryan is haunted by the urgent question of how they will sustain themselves as the water supply dwindles and record-breaking temperatures set in. The limited stock of non-perishable food is rapidly diminishing, fueling a desperate need to kickstart their reconstruction efforts.

With Cecilia's parents still missing, Ryan embarks on a perilous mission to reunite their fractured family. Entrusting his friend Steve with the responsibilities in Harper Springs, he sets out with his father towards Fox Lake, only to encounter a series of harrowing obstacles that surpass the terror of tornadoes. Blazing wildfires, towering walls of dirt, and the ever-present threat of ruthless thieves and looters turn their journey into a battle for survival. As they bear witness to the widespread devastation and a post-apocalyptic landscape, they realize the daunting truth—the road to recovery may be more treacherous than they ever imagined.

Get ready for a relentless rollercoaster ride through a world torn apart by extreme weather, as the characters face the harshest tests of their lives. Will they find the strength and ingenuity to rebuild against all odds, or will they succumb to the unforgiving forces of a damaged climate, forever lost in a post-apocalyptic wasteland?

WANT MORE NATURAL DISASTER THRILLERS?

Beneath a turbulent sky, two meteorologists find themselves at the forefront of a cataclysmic battle between humanity and nature in this gripping tale of survival. Gavin Dolan and Avery Phillips, seasoned storm chasers, have witnessed the fury of hurricanes and tornadoes firsthand. But nothing could prepare them for the monstrous storm systems threatening to annihilate mankind.

As the world teeters on the brink of devastation, Gavin and Avery are thrust into a race against time. The government turns to them for answers, tasking them with unraveling the mysteries behind these unprecedented weather phenomena. Lives hang in the balance as each new storm unleashes a deadly dance of destruction, pitting humanity's resilience against the wrath of the elements.

In this war waged on a grand scale, families are torn apart, communities shattered, and the very fabric of civilization unravels. With dwindling resources and desperate stakes, Gavin and Avery must delve into the depths of scientific knowledge to comprehend the origins of these apocalyptic weather patterns. Yet, as they uncover shocking truths, they face a haunting realization—nature is gearing up for its ultimate revenge, poised to reclaim what was once taken for granted and usher in the extinction of the human race.

Amid the chaos, Gavin and Avery must summon their expertise, courage, and unyielding determination to defy the unfathomable forces of nature. Can they unlock the secrets that lie within the tempests' heart and find a way to preserve humanity's existence? Or will they become mere witnesses to the earth's wrathful retribution?

In this gripping tale of suspense and survival, the boundaries of human ingenuity are tested against the overwhelming power of nature. Brace yourself for an electrifying journey as Gavin and Avery navigate a world teetering on the edge of annihilation, where the ultimate question looms: Can humanity outwit its own demise and weather the storm of a lifetime?

ACKNOWLEDGMENTS

I would like to thank my mother for always sticking by my side. I know it's not easy being around a writer. My constant chit-chat about ideas drives her crazy, but she always supports me and encourages me to push ahead and keep going. I also can't forget you readers. I love sharing my stories with you. You are my inspiration, and the driving force for me to continue down this path of creativity. Even if I only hear back from one of you, it makes all of the time and effort I put into this all worth every ounce of effort I give. Thank you, to each and every one of you out there!

CONTACT INFORMATION

Join my mailing list to get updates on new releases! No spam will be sent!

http://eepurl.com/byKpRb

Email:
JTateAuthor@yahoo.com

Website:
https://jtateauthor.wixsite.com/jrtate

TikTok:
JRTateAuthor

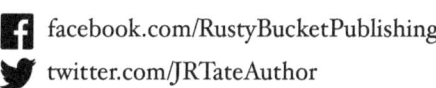 facebook.com/RustyBucketPublishing

twitter.com/JRTateAuthor

instagram.com/j.r.tateauthor

ABOUT THE AUTHOR

J.R. Tate is an accomplished author based in Texas, where she draws inspiration from the breathtaking landscapes and the spirit of resilience that permeates the region. With a passion for nature and adventure, she often explores the great outdoors, hiking through scenic trails and finding solace in the mountains. These experiences lend an authentic touch to her writing, bringing the settings and landscapes to life with vivid detail.

Beyond her literary pursuits, she also works as a social-emotional counselor, dedicated to helping children navigate their emotions and behaviors. Her background in counseling provides her with a deep understanding of the human psyche, which shines through in her compelling character portrayals and exploration of complex emotions.

As an author, J.R. captivates readers with her engaging storytelling and immersive writing style. She seamlessly weaves together elements of suspense, adventure, and human drama, creating narratives that keep readers on the edge of their seats. With each page, she delves into the depths of her characters' hearts, unearthing their fears, hopes, and desires, and inviting readers to embark on emotional journeys alongside them.

Her commitment to crafting compelling stories is matched only by her dedication to authenticity and attention to detail. Her ability to capture the essence of the human experience in the face of adversity resonates deeply with readers, leaving a lasting impact long after they turn the final page.

With her unique blend of adventure, heartfelt emotion, and a keen understanding of the human condition, she is an author to watch. Her stories transport readers to captivating worlds, exploring the triumphs and tribulations of her characters in a way that leaves a lasting impression.

Made in United States
Troutdale, OR
07/12/2023